FIFTEEN STORIES TO HOME

Fifteen Stories to Home

A collection of short stories

by

JONATHAN MANISCALCO

BOOKS

Adelaide Books
New York / Lisbon
2020

FIFTEEN STORIES TO HOME
A collection of short stories
By Jonathan Maniscalco

Copyright © by Jonathan Maniscalco
Cover design © 2020 Adelaide Books

Published by Adelaide Books, New York / Lisbon
adelaidebooks.org

Editor-in-Chief
Stevan V. Nikolic

For any information, please address Adelaide Books
at info@adelaidebooks.org

or write to:

Adelaide Books
244 Fifth Ave. Suite D27
New York, NY, 10001

ISBN: 978-1-953510-83-9

Printed in the United States of America

Contents

Gone Again

They only held hands loosely while walking down the platform, but he didn't want to let go. At his train-car he stopped to say goodbye, biting down on his cheeks to maintain dignity. She was neither indifferent nor cold, but she also wasn't unhappy.

"You'll call me when you get there?" She asked, modestly.

He nodded, feeling some of the hot tears burning around the eyes of his winter scorched face.

"Yeah, I'll message you." He managed to say, clearly, while he rubbed his eyes as if it was the wind stinging them.

"Ok," She replied.

He kissed her and said he'd miss her. She reciprocated both gestures and squeezed his hands. Feeling there was nothing else to say, he picked up his bag and got on the train.

He saw her waving through the window when he found his seat. After waving back happily, he put the small carry-on, filled with his life, in the overhead. When he looked back out. She wasn't there.

Disappointed, he sat down, putting his backpack between his legs. Then he stared out and tried to imagine her there again. Making his mind try and form the already pixelating memory where she had been, while he again felt the embarrassing heat around his eyes and down his cheeks.

He was going again. Leaving another life behind for the sake of living it to the fullest, experiencing new exciting things through immersion in foreign life with no commitment. He was going, again. Newness was starting to seem the same. Reflection on his transience now only caused his mind to fill with the inevitable thoughts of what might have been. He could have been happy anywhere. He could have been happy with here, or there, but mainly, he could have been happy with her. Instead, it was always never long before he was gone again.

Suddenly tired, he closed his eyes and seemingly on cue, the train started moving, taking him away from what was really new.

There were two suitcases. One large and another that could be strapped on while he rolled it through the airport. In these two bags were everything he needed and wanted. Ryan also had a backpack that had his most personal items. He pulled the handle out from the larger bag and walked out of his bedroom. It was time to go. He could wait for Andrew to pick him up outside.

Going Away

Ryan Clarke was twenty-two years old.

It was a warm night outside. One for going out and celebrating. It was nice of Bernardo to organize his going-away party. Ryan knew he should show his appreciation with participation, so he got up off the hotel bed and walked out onto the balcony where Bernardo, Andrew, and Beck were drinking and looking out at the city.

"There he is," Bernardo said, happily handing Ryan one of the beers they had smuggled into the room.

"This place is really fucking big." Beck said to the group. "The city you're going to is even bigger, right Ryan?"

"The one I'm landing in," Ryan replied. He took a sip from his beer. "But I'm only there for orientation, then I'm being bussed out to a smaller city, more out in the center of the country."

The group was quiet for a minute, each of their biases imagining the journey across a foreign landscape.

"This is a really nice view guys." Ryan said, drinking the beer quickly. Then adding, "It must have been a lot?"

"Don't worry about it." Bernardo answered. "You have an expensive ass flight on a new credit card. And besides, you just would've had to transfer here from Boston anyway so you might as well buy the ticket here.

"Okay fine," Ryan replied, taking another beer from Bernardo. "I've never been to New York."

"None of us have." Andrew said, also taking a new beer. "So have you gotten all your thoughts out of the way now that you're off the bed?"

"Mostly I guess." Ryan replied. "I don't know."

"It's a big move." Bernardo said.

"But like, if you don't like it you can always come back." Andrew said. "I'll spot you a ticket."

"Thanks, I know. But I don't know." Ryan was mumbling slightly. "The contract is just a year. I don't think I'll quit."

"That's not that long." Andrew agreed. "They're giving you pretty nice renewal bonus though, right?"

Ryan nodded, smiling. "Yeah, the completion bonuses are pretty good too."

"So it would be pretty good if you liked it out there."

"It would, for other reasons too."

"Obviously,"

"You two sound too sad." Bernardo said, a hint of desperation in his voice.

"I'm sorry." Ryan replied, forcing out a laugh. "So what do you guys want to do tonight?"

"We haven't really thought about it." Bernardo laughed. "We were thinking of walking around the area near NYU."

"That sounds good." Ryan said.

"Did you want to go to a club? Or something?" Andrew asked.

"Not really, I have an afternoon flight, but even then I don't want to be hurting badly on that level tomorrow."

"Yeah, I'm glad. That's not really my kind of place." Beck said.

"Why not?" Ryan laughed. "You're too cool for what's cool?"

"More like I hate putting on nice clothes."

"You country fuck," Ryan laughed, which Bernard joined when he saw Andrew and Beck were too.

"So we go to a few bars?" Ryan asked. "Maybe throw up in Washington Square Park?"

"Is that enough?" Bernardo asked.

Ryan nodded. "I don't need much man, thanks for putting this together."

"We need dinner too." Andrew said. "I've already drank too many beers on an empty stomach."

"We could get pizza," Beck replied. "We're in New York."

"We're also close to K-Town though."

"The fuck is K-Town?"

"Korea-town, it's like China-town but Korean."

"Is Korean food any good? I don't think I've ever had it."

"Fucking bomb," Ryan said, and Bernardo nodded.

"Shit why aren't you moving there?"

Ryan shrugged, "Maybe next one."

"How many beers are left?" Andrew asked, just before finishing another.

"Six," Bernardo replied.

"You guys get two each. I've been hogging them."

"What's your fucking rush?" Ryan asked with a smile. "We can stay out all night in this city."

"Maybe I want to be the one to vom in that park first." Andrew said with a tinge of nervousness to the joke.

The time before they went out was more joking with each other with periodical staring out at the dark twinkling city. They all liked the river. It was like all rivers, always going forward to somewhere. Ryan and Bernardo also saw their lesser one in it, while the other two just liked it because it was something familiar in the wilderness of lights, people, and concrete overstimulating the standards that had molded their relative understanding of quantity.

After finishing the beers, they left together and crossed the avenues guided by their phones past Times Square to one of the other streets brighter at night than the day. None of them knew where to eat so they just picked one that made them the most comfortable.

"So do you like Korean food?" Bernardo asked after.

"Yeah, man," Beck answered. "I think I'm sold. Too bad there's nowhere for it on Cape."

"Sort of the way it is for most things." Andrew mumbled. He had had some rice wine with dinner and was feeling woozy.

"How long a walk is it to NYU?" Ryan asked.

"Twenty minutes," Bernardo replied. "Do you want to like see the buildings or just want me to find a bar?"

"Just find a bar, then we'll walk around after we've drank a little more."

"Every street looks the fucking same." Beck said as they walked downtown. "If the streets weren't numbered, I'd get lost immediately."

"That's the point." Andrew laughed. Stumbling a little and grabbing Ryan's shoulder.

"It's just block after block of the same thing."

"Concrete jungle!" Andrew yelled.

"How do you stand out at all? It's fucking suffocating. I'd blow my fucking brains out here."

"I get that." Ryan said.

"Is that why you're going to a foreign country?" Beck asked. "To stand out?"

"Sort of, but more like to stand out to myself."

"What does that mean?"

"I dunno."

"Shit's going to be crazy out there." Bernardo said. "Maybe we should've gone to karaoke back in K-Town."

"Nah, I'll do that over there. I'll have a last night with you guys doing what we like to do."

"Getting drunk and wandering?" Bernardo asked.

Ryan shrugged again, "That's good dude."

"Okay," Bernardo smiled and gripped the shoulder Andrew wasn't leaning on.

They came to the bar Bernardo had picked. It was a place trying to look dive-y before you saw the prices and noticed the clientele through the dim lighting after going downstairs to a small space filled with round tables propped up by barrels.

Andrew had water and the rest of them had beers on tap. The tables were filled. Ryan caught his eyes panning lazily over the group at each table. There were mostly men. In every group they were the majority and made up the entirety of some.

"Seems like what a bar would be like around NYU." Andrew mumbled, rubbing his face.

"I wonder how long this place has been around." Another friend said. Ryan wasn't listening. The other groups all fit *American* personalities, but maybe they had universality that Ryan just didn't know. It was probably a mixed bag. But maybe he'd have a better idea of what that meant if he was ever sitting here again.

"Do you think we order at the bar like before?" Andrew asked.

"Probably," Bernardo said, "You want the same kind I had? I was about to go up."

Andrew nodded and Beck put in the same request which prompted Ryan to follow Bernardo to the bar.

"How're you doing?"

"I'm fine man, you don't have to keep asking."

"Sorry man."

"Don't worry," Ryan laughed, shoving Bernardo's slightly. "I'm having a good time. I've just got shit on my mind."

"What did your parents say last night?"

"That they loved me."

"Well, yeah."

"Also that they were proud of me and hoped I liked it."

"Think they'll visit?"

"Maybe my mom, I don't know when my dad would be able to."

"Have to stay out there a little longer for him." Bernardo smiled.

"I guess I do." Ryan said. "And for you, too."

Bernardo smiled again and picked up two of the beers that had been placed in front of them.

Ryan picked up the other two, then turned to find himself getting stared down by a man a little younger, but bigger than him. Wearing a red Brook Brother's plaid with expensive black jeans, and dress shoes he had bought to look casual. His face looked ready to fight while the rest seem more ready to go shopping in Boulder.

"You okay?" Ryan asked.

"I think you need to stop staring." The guy barked.

Bernardo coughed up some of the beer he had been sipping.

Ryan raised an eyebrow and sipped his own beer, waiting for the guy to continue.

"Staring at what exactly?" Bernardo asked through a chuckle.

"The girls," The guy snapped, trying to get into a staring contest with Ryan, which he was ignoring.

"What girls?" Bernardo asked.

"The ones at our table. Your friend keeps staring at them." His voice wasn't as confident at Bernardo.

"Okay dude," Ryan said, pushing through. "I won't look in your girlfriend's direction again."

"She's not my girlfriend. I just don't want you looking at any of them." He barked, knocking Ryan with his shoulder, which spilled the beer.

"What the fuck, bro. He wasn't doing anything, get over your fucking-self." Bernardo yelled, slamming the beers back down on the bar, spilling the top third all over his hands and the bar top.

"I didn't mean to do that." The guy cried, throwing his hands up defensively.

Ryan gave this guy a second look before he examined how wet the spill had made his shirt. Looking past the nice clothes and smooth spoiled features he saw a punk. Less dangerous and angry than the typical kind, the bad behavior instead facilitated through brattiness pretending to be indignation.

"It's fine." Ryan said, pinching his wet shirt between his fingers. "Let's just go."

He put his now half-empty beers on the bar next to Bernardo's and walked out.

"I'm sorry you paid for beers none of us drank." Ryan said to Bernardo once they were outside.

"It's nothing dude, just four beers. Fuck that guy though, whatever the fuck he was talking about. Why didn't you kick his teeth in? I thought he was fucking done when he made you spill the beers.

"Yeah, I just wasn't into it. Want to find a liquor store and mix some whiskey with soda?"

"Then I'm fucked." Andrew said, his voice still slurred.

"Let's get fucked." Ryan chuckled. "Then we'll go to the park."

Liquor stores were everywhere so it only took fifteen minutes to make their simple concoction and be standing under the arch with 12oz bottles in their hands.

"So this is it, huh?" Andrew said. He wasn't drinking from his bottle and seemed less inebriated to Ryan.

"Yeah, I've seen it in movies. Looks more or less the same." Ryan said. "There's more people around though. I think we're in the way of a lot of pictures."

"Maybe it's better to look at if you go to NYU." Bernardo said.

"Probably, I like the area around the JFK Museum." Ryan said.

"You aren't drinking, dude." Beck said to Andrew.

"I don't actually want to throw up and make Ryan take care of me the night before he leaves the country."

"Well, I'd ask them to do it." Ryan said, nodding at Bernardo and Beck.

"Right, but you know what I mean."

"Yeah, you're feeling better though?"

"I think I'm good now."

"You really can't see anything outside of this park." Beck said.

"You mean aside from the building's surrounding us?"

"Yeah,"

"There's a plane." Ryan said, looking directly up.

"Shit, you're right." Beck said. "That'll be you tomorrow."

Ryan nodded as he watched the blinking light in the sky go over them and disappear behind the tall pillars with irregularly lit windows. That would be him tomorrow, going somewhere he really only knew the name of. This city was different. Bigger, louder, and brighter than anything he ever seen, but still his home. Only turned up to a higher volume. Tomorrow he wouldn't have that comfort.

The guy from the bar probably went here. Ryan had assumed he was an NYU student. But even if he wasn't, this was a popular enough spot. He'd probably avoid him and his friends if he came walking through and saw them here. Ryan would let him too. Like at the bar, he couldn't bring himself to care about false bravado.

The whole thing was a tired waste of time. He wasn't going to do something to keep him here when he had somewhere to go.

"Thanks for coming down here with me, guys," Ryan said, slowly unscrewing his cap and taking a drink. "You're who I wanted around tonight."

As they all said how happy they were to be with him. Ryan looked at his friends, knowing they were hoping he'd tell them what he wanted to do next. But in that moment he was truly content.

The plane was large, but Ryan still didn't have much room. He was worried that after he fell asleep he'd wake up with cramps from the tight area. It was a long flight so it couldn't be helped.

It didn't matter anyway.

Gone

In his excitement he had arrived at the airport too early. Two hours before a flight wasn't too bad. He wasn't bored or anxious and it was nice to have dumped his big bag and just walk around with a backpack. It had been a heavy bag but it wasn't much considering it was everything he was bringing from what he had already designated as his old life.

Very little in this bag was truly personal. Its weight came from clothes and other possessions from his old life that would wear out over time and be replaced as his new self culminated.

He'd soon be changed for the better. Immersed in the culture he knew he was most designed for, an environment where there could only be benefits. He knew he had been born in the wrong place and that had of course stifled him. It wasn't too late to make the correction. And with this correction he'd learn and adjust. Then he'd fit in. Something he had never done back home. He had always been an outcast even before he had discovered why. Thinking he had been defective and destined to be out of place and lonely. But now he had found where he could live his life to the fullest. All that was needed now was to get there.

He was at his Gate. His flight wasn't even being shown on the screen above the desk. He had his old book in the big pocket of his coat. The only thing he was bringing that would be painful to replace. He had read it a million times. The story was only from a few generations ago, but feeling the different culture and history in its eastern narrative standing out in every aspect would always be a fresh memory. It had been the spark that had lit his drive to go abroad. Not the spark to leave, that had been there for as long as he could remember. Regardless. Now he was gone and he wouldn't be sad about leaving anything behind.

This airport was clean, but still the same. The products he had always seen hiding behind different brands and cuter mascots. Still, the cleanliness was a nice change. The people around him mostly mirrored the country he was in, but there were enough people around with his face that he hadn't really started to stand out yet.

Boar Hunt

The bush was a prickly uneven bed to lay on. Still, William was comfortable. The old butcher was on the bush next him with his eyes half open and the rifle across his belly. It had gotten warmer since the sun had come up but the wind chilled the air. The two of them had been at this spot on the hill for a long time, looking lazily over the plains littered with patches of tall grass and trees for several miles up to the mountains. It was a clear day so the snowcapped peaks were visible.

The prospect of hunting had not excited him when his host father had explained that was going to be the first activity of his new European life. He wasn't against the practice, but held the common suburban distaste and overall squeamishness towards it. This was nice though. The view was not only beautiful but served as a contrast to the fields of shining wheat he had seen the way up here and an addition to the collage his mind was making of this country.

It was all new so he should try things he wouldn't back home. He wasn't going to shoot anything anyway.

They sat longer. When dogs started barking in the distance the butcher jumped up with agility beyond his age and shape. William started to get up, but the large hand of the butcher hovering above kept him down. The barking was still distant.

Lifting his rifle, the butcher looked through the scope and aimed. Squinting, William tried to see what he was pointing at, but couldn't. The rifle went off a second later and William caught a small dot moving across the frosty grass. A pack of smaller dots were gaining on the slowing first dot, but before they caught it William was pulled up by the butcher and the two jumped off the hill to where their doorless jeep had been waiting. The butcher drove, seeming to know exactly where his target was going to end up. After twists and turns they came out of a tree patch to see the dogs had surrounded a boar. They were attacking all at once. The boar kept them back with its big tusks, which regulated the hounds' bites to its legs and back side whenever it turned its back on a new section of the circle.

Two other jeeps had arrived before them. One of which had contained William's host father. He was standing over the circle of dogs with the hunters from the other jeeps. His big body in his coat and a mud-flap hat on his head with both hands clutching a similar rifle to the butcher. The barking from the dogs had not ceased in their attack. Now accompanied with snarls that barred their teeth ferociously and dripped with eager saliva. The boar's tusks were lowering and the dogs were getting bolder, biting at its face and jumping on its back.

The brutality of it was hard for William to watch. The crumbling boar wasn't satiating the dogs' bloodlust but intensifying it. Their barks turned to howls as they piled on top of the wild animal, biting deeper and longer until it stopped twitching. One of the hunters without a gun ran up to the dogs shouting and waving his arms. The dogs bounced off the boar in different directions and started dancing around their trainer howling and jumping with a primal happiness William had never seen in a dog back home. But whatever wholesome dignity William could take from that was ruined when the trainer grabbed the tusks of their kill and started waving it around. It seemed unnecessary and against what William had been taught the relationship hunters and prey should have from the lore of his country's noble, almost mythical, hunters. Still, the animal was dead and it was making the dogs happy. These were actual hunters.

Another trainer was kneeling in front of a lone dog off to the side of the commotion. William could tell the dog was hurt by its whining. The trainer was rubbing salve on the large gash near its mouth and whispering reassurances as the dog twitched away.

William felt more for the dog than the boar. He thought he shouldn't but something natural was pulling him to appreciate the sacrifice the dog had made more than the boar's life.

Another gun sounded and echoed over them. The dogs looked up at the sky, then at their trainer, who started yelling and waving his hands again. The dogs took off and everyone but William spoke in rapid Basque before jumping to their newly designated task. William's host father and a trainer got in a jeep and drove in the direction the dogs had gone. The trainer who had treated the dog picked the wounded animal up and was driven in a different direction by another hunter.

It was just William, the butcher, and the boar.

The butcher took out plastic gloves a doctor would use from his pocket. He put them on and unsheathed the knife attached to his pant leg. He looked over at the boar then at William. Deciding something, he took out another pair of gloves from his pocket and handed them to William.

William put them on without thinking about it, but backed away surprised when he realized the butcher was handing him the knife. The butcher smiled widely and nodded vigorously. William took the dull handle and stared at the butcher as he started speaking quickly and making cutting motions. William looked at the edge of the blade and nodded. Bending over the dead boar, William unhappily touched the tip of the knife to its stomach. It felt tender and soft beneath the dark hair. He looked at the butcher, who nodded enthusiastically. Feeling trapped, William pushed the knife into the dead animal expecting disgust or nausea.

He didn't feel any though. The knife had gone in easily and emotionlessly like he had cut into a dummy or mannequin. With barely any effort, William dragged the knife down the rest of the belly. The flesh opened on each side as the knife slid down, releasing a wheezing sound as gas escaped the body. When he was done, William was looking down at an assortment of guts he believed to be similar to his own. In his peripheral, William saw the butcher making a lifting motion and William stuck the knife back in the boar and started lifting the wet, squishy, putrid smelling, guts out of the animal and leaving it next to the boar as a lucky surprise for fouler animals. When he was finished, the butcher patted his back before flipping the boar over. Blood soaked the frosted tipped grass a dark ugly red. When it was over, William helped the butcher carry the boar by the legs and laid it on the towels in the back of the jeep. Pointing to a bag in the back, the butchers took his gloves off and put them into it. William did the same.

They drove back to the church that had been the meeting spot in the early morning and where the town ended. Not long after, William's host father returned with another boar. Later, his host family, the butcher's family, and many more people from the town gathered around the church's outdoor tables for a picnic.

The dogs were playing with the children. Running after and pouncing aggressively on the sticks and balls they threw, barking. A noise that whether excited or angry had lost its innocence to William.

William's host father called him over to the grill he was cooking over. He handed William a meat sandwich, which he knew would taste better before biting because now it was less abstract and had been earned. Even if how it had come about had been ugly. Meat would always taste like food in a newly satisfying way to William.

Of course this wasn't the boar he had cut. His was still laying in the trunk to be further prepared for consumption at the butcher's *carniceria*.

Checked in, Ryan looked out the window of the hotel. The buildings were a different shape than he was used to. They were of course still tall rectangles, but with a smoothness to their design that almost made the sides and points seem to have a roundness. It was early in the morning here and the other new worker from the company was snoring in the bed next to him. For Ryan it was the middle of the afternoon. He wouldn't have been able to sleep anyway.

Welcome Party

Ryan Clarke was twenty three-years old.

The basement of the restaurant was dimly lit, giving the other workers of Ryan's prefecture a level of mystery across the long table. On his right was Brendan, another American and fellow teacher at his school. On his left was a teacher from a different school. And in front of him were two more from Northern England. The main dishes hadn't been brought out yet and everyone was talking in small groups while eating edamame and drinking beer or rice wine.

"I'm not kidding. I'm ready for Tokyo." The teacher on Ryan's left said, mostly to the two British teachers. "I tried the whole *real Japan* thing out here, but I need to get back to the city."

"When do you leave?" Asked the British teacher on Ryan's left. He was short and slightly heavyset with a face Ryan associated more with the people he had grown up with than what he'd imagined the English looked like.

"Next week, I have a gig at a club the night after." He answered.

"Are you a musician or a DJ or something?" Ryan asked.

"Pretty sure they're the same thing, and yeah." The other teacher replied, looking at Ryan with offense clearly taken.

"I'm sorry." Ryan said, not really caring. He looked at the two British teachers and asked to remind him of their names. He couldn't remember the other teacher's name either.

"Shane, mate," Said the one who had asked the other teacher when he was leaving.

"I'm Daniel." Said the teacher next to Shane. He was tall and much thinner than Shane, but wasn't very muscular. His hair was lighter and his facial features were more of what Ryan would think of as traditionally British. They were both drinking light colored beers and appeared to be close.

"You're pretty new here right?" Shane said. "You weren't at the last work party."

Ryan nodded. "Yeah, been here three weeks. The only other teachers I know are Brendan and Andrew. Well, I know Kasumi too, but she isn't a teacher."

"Nice," Shane said, laughing and smiling. "Been here a month and a half. It's good to have another new guy around. I was tired of being surrounded by only veterans like him." He nodded at Daniel.

"How long have you been here?" Ryan asked Daniel.

"Six months," Daniel said, smiling. "He's sort of kidding but the first few does make a big difference."

"We came in the same group." Brendan said, sipping his tea. Brendan didn't drink.

"And you've been here a year?" Ryan asked the DJ, giving him another chance.

He nodded. "Yup, and once I started to get close to the end of my contract I opted for a new one."

"Because you wanted to get back to the city." Ryan said. "Have you lived in Tokyo before or do you mean back to a city in general?"

"Never lived in Tokyo," He replied, leaning back, "I'm excited to see what kind of opportunities it has."

"So did you ever DJ in New York or Miami or somewhere like that before you came here?" Ryan asked, with a little interest.

The other teacher shifted his lip to one side instead of answering. Then looked at Shane and Daniel saying, "Americans right?"

Both Shane and Daniel seemed surprised by this statement. The other teacher didn't seem to notice, looking back at Ryan and finally answering with, "I'm Canadian. I'm used to gigs in Toronto and I've done a few in Vancouver too. We have our own cities."

Ryan didn't feel like apologizing again so in a voice with a casual tone to mask his more aggressive feelings, said, "You shouldn't get mad at me for thinking you were getting work in bigger cities."

Shane and Daniel inhaled, both surprised and amused. Ryan heard Brendan chuckle beside him.

"Toronto is a big enough city all by itself." The Canadian teacher said with a little venom he wasn't afraid of showing, "Maybe if you Americans knew anything about other countries you'd know that."

"Mhmm," Ryan murmured, "We're known to be that way. I've never been to Toronto, but I've never been to LA either and only been to New York once and I'm aware they're bigger. I didn't mean to offend you."

The last part was genuine. Ryan's annoyance was fighting with his brain reminding him that he needed to make a good impression around these people, even the ones who were leaving.

"It's alright." The Canadian teacher replied. "You get used to Americans being like that. Even your nationality makes you guys think you're the only people on Earth. *Americans,* like there's only one country in North and South America."

"Yeah, it can be a little awkward." Ryan said, his annoyance starting to overtake his resolve again.

From the other end of the table, Ryan's regional coordinator began an address to all of them.

"Could everyone please take a moment for an announcement." The manager started, lifting his small glass that was shaped like a large thimble. He was British too, but had a more refined accent than Shane and Daniel. His nose was red. "The food is coming out soon and I wanted to get this little announcement over with before we start eating rather than after." The long table became politely silent. "First, I'd like to welcome our new teachers Ryan, David, Sean, and Andrea." Ryan instinctively raised his hand and peered up and down the table to see who the other new teachers were. "Also, I'm sorry to say that we have some teachers leaving us as well. So this is also partly to say goodbye to Gregory, Matt, Sean, Kyle, and Timothy. Thank you all for your service here, we hope you had an enriching experience, and have a good trip back home. And Kyle, have a wonderful time in Tokyo."

Everyone then lifted their various glasses and shouted a word reminiscent of *cheers*. Ryan followed a second behind.

The food started coming around after the speech. It was chicken or beef on sticks, popular here as an after-work food to have with beer.

"So why did you come to Japan?" Kyle asked Ryan as he picked up a piece of chicken. "And how long are you going to stay here?"

"I wanted something different. And I don't know." Ryan said, shortly. "What about you?"

"The music industry is bought and sold. Thanks again to your country." Kyle replied, taking a bite off his stick. "It doesn't let artists express themselves unless it can make a quick buck. So I can't support myself on my art alone back home." Then adopting a more instructive voice said, "But I'm also a buddhist so I'm very spiritual. I decided to take this as an opportunity to get in better touch with the meta-physical world."

"How's that been going?" Daniel asked in an amused tone.

"I'm disappointed. This country's spirituality has been ruined and replaced by the USA's corporatocracy. That's what they worship now."

"I don't think he likes us very much." Ryan said, turning to Brendan, whose uncomfortable face smiled a little.

"No, it's not your fault." Kyle said, in a merciful tone. "Your country's full of hypocrisies like that. Like your name and…"

"How you call American football just football and football, soccer." Shane cut in. He had a toothy smile on his face.

"Well the game used to be called gridiron-football, but it just got shortened. I think." Ryan looked at Brendan and asked, "That is right, right?"

Brendan shrugged.

"Sorry," Ryan laughed. "I assumed you'd know, being from Texas."

"It's not a bad guess." Brendan said, smiling. I'm just not into sports in general."

"Don't all Americans love American football?" Kyle asked. "What does being from Texas matter?"

"They like it more." Ryan answered, dismissively. "There's three hundred million of us, not all the regions are going to be the same."

"Anyway," Kyle continued. "What I was going to say was your country's hypocrisy is thinking you're the only free nation on earth. Like you guys just legalized gay marriage a few years ago. That's like a basis of freedom. Being with who you want."

"Pretty sure my state legalized it before Canada." Ryan sighed.

"When?"

"03', maybe 04', I can't remember. I was sort of young."

"Where are you from?"

"Massachusetts, it's the state where Boston is."

"I know that."

"Well you didn't know Texans liked football."

"I didn't know they liked football more."

"Same thing,"

"No it's not. Knowing where some place is that's close to Canada and knowing what one obscure part of your country likes is different."

"His State's population is practically your country's." Ryan growled.

He could feel Brendan was uncomfortable.

"So I guess we don't matter then." Kyle snapped a little loudly. "That's what I've been talking about this whole time."

"Yeah, I really never said that." Ryan said, putting his elbows on the table and glaring at Kyle.

Kyle stiffened a little and Ryan remembered what other people were like and put his hands back in his lap.

"It's just what you're taught." Kyle said. "That's what I've been trying to tell you. Like I bet you were taught the USA won World War II."

"Did we lose, actually?" Ryan said, sarcastically.

"No, but you weren't the only country to fight. Canada took a beach by itself in Normandy. I bet you didn't learn that in history class."

"I'm aware Canadians fought in World War II." Ryan said, putting a fist into his cheek, "Thing is, I'd rather not talk about a war that was fought against the country I'm in. Especially when I've just gotten here."

"And because it's almost August?" Kyle asked, snickering. "Feeling a little guilty?"

His eyes widening in surprise. Ryan pushed his fist deeper into his cheek, but instead of further provoking him, the extremity of the comment pacified his mind to thinking too little of this person to reply.

"That's a little much Kyle." Shane barked, while raising his hand for another beer. "Can you not hear you're being a right cunt?"

Shamed for a second, Kyle turned pink before recovering and saying. "I love that word. It's not really used in Canada, what I mean by that is that it's taboo." Then unable to help himself nodded his head at Ryan and said, "Offends this guy's sensibilities."

Ryan shifted his eyes over, his fist still digging into his check, to look at Brendan again and say in a tired voice, "Like I said, I don't think he likes us very much."

The laughter at the table satiated Ryan enough for the evening.

Later, Ryan was sitting next to Brendan on the train back to the city at the west end of their prefecture where they lived.

"That guy Kyle was a real fucking asshole." Ryan said, bluntly.

"Yeah," Brendan said, "He's very opinionated."

"I'm sorry if I made you uncomfortable." Ryan said, diffused a little. "I was trying to not let him bother me, but a few times I let him get to me. Like he's not even wrong in some ways. But like what am I supposed to do about it?"

"You were better than a lot of other people." Brendan said. "Last party he and Shane got into it about the Queen. The administration here might be happy to see him go."

"So he's not typical here? That kind of personality I mean."

Brendan rocked his head back and forth.

"I wouldn't say he's typical, but he isn't rare either. People who go aboard are sometimes like that or I think even become like that once they get out here. I've met a few like him and I haven't been here really that long."

"He should probably go back to Canada." Ryan said.

"Unless he left because he's like that over there too." Brendan mumbled.

They were silent a moment.

"I guess this job might attract misfits." Ryan said. "That's a scary thought."

Brendan shrugged. "I'd try to become friends with some locals. You'll learn more like that, anyway."

His home was small. When Ryan would walk into his apartment he'd first go down a short hallway where his kitchen, refrigerator, and bathroom were. The hallway opened up into a living room that couldn't fit a couch, so he made due with only a chair and a table to eat at. Along the wall where the hallway ended was a ladder that brought him up to the cubby that was his bedroom. He had to be as economical as possible.

A Full Day

He had enjoyed the show and she had enjoyed it much more. It was evident in how excitedly she was chatting away about it with the friends of Angela's cousin. He didn't feel a need to participate. His novice Spanish would slow the conversation down. He was happy she was so enough to tell these strangers. She was usually very shy.

"So, did you like it?" Angela's cousin asked, sitting in a similar kitchen chair as him on his right.

He replied that he had, joking that he might've liked it almost half as much as his two co-workers. That made her laugh and softly bite down on her lip. Angela's cousin was attractive in a sensual way. Her body was thin and curvy. Her speech quick and deliberate, contrasted by movements that were slow and delicate. Her clothes created an image of a more seductive 1970's, covering her conservatively when still, but revealing with even minor movements causing him to uncomfortably look away. Angela's cousin was probably struggling as much as he was with the Spanish being spoken. And like him, and every other American in the apartment, had come to Spain to improve her aspiring second language. Madrid probably put her in these situations often. He was glad he hadn't been placed in the city. It was too easy to cheat and situations like this seemed to happen more often than in the countryside. Madrid was fast like New York and London, where people tended to bring that speed into every part of life.

As if reading his mind, Angela's cousin asked, "Were you able to follow the whole thing?"

He held up his hand with his fingers stretched and rotated it back and forth. "It definitely helped that I knew the story going in."

"Think I'd be okay then?"

"Oh totally, I heard you speaking when I got here. You're a notch above me, so I'm sure you'd be fine."

After nodding at his answer, Angela's cousin asked. "So how do you like Madrid?"

"I don't know." He replied, laughing. "I only got here a few hours ago. We barely had time to get to the city, check into the hotel, and cab it to the theater. I haven't had a chance to see the city at all."

"Oh, that's kind of exciting! It's still a mystery. What do you want to see?"

"Well the palace is supposed to be nice." He replied. "And right next to it is that Cathedral so that's a good area to go first. Then maybe we can go to the Museum Arte Reina Sofía. But at night though, I think I want to walk around the Botanical Garden. We're staying right by it and it looks like there's a Christmas faire. That could be nice."

"That last part will be cute." Angela's cousin said, with a smile that revealed just her upper teeth.

"Yeah," He said, feeling his cheeks get a little hot.

"It sounds like you have a full day tomorrow." Angela's cousin said, continuing to smile. Then leaning in closer and lowering her voice asked, "So did you two meet in the program?"

"Yeah," He replied, looking slightly to the right of her. "It actually started near the beginning of the semester when we went to Ireland together. We both needed someone to go with. So we went as friends and came back… As not…"

Angela's cousin pursed her lips, "That's really cute. But…" She paused, then continued, "I'm surprised you didn't end up with a Spanish woman."

"All the ones in my little town are married already." He replied, in a playfully automatic tone.

"Oh, so she was what was available?"

"Stop it." He said, laughing. "That's not what I meant."

"I know. I'm just kidding. It's not a rule we have to get with Spaniards anyway."

"It probably helps with learning the language though."

"You don't seem bothered."

"Yeah, I'm really happy." He said, looking directly at her.

She raised an eyebrow, "You two look really good together. Does she help you with your Spanish?"

He nodded, "Yeah, she helps a lot."

"See, that's still useful. Is she a native speaker?"

"No," He laughed. "And she's mad at her parents about it. Her grandparents are immigrants and she got a little from them. And she says so many people in Texas speaking Spanish helps too."

He felt a head softly land on his shoulder before Angela's cousin could respond. "Que decís?" She asked, looking up at him with her deep, dark brown eyes.

"He's speaking your graces." Angela's cousin answered for him, leaning back in her chair. "I think you got him on the hook."

She turned red and lifted her head. "Stop, he's not, is he?"

Angela's cousin put her index finger close to her thumb and winked.

He put an arm around her and even though she was embarrassed, nuzzled into him.

The evening went on. When someone decided it was time to go out, they got up together and put on coats before walking out of the apartment and then the building. It was new. Built in the same brightly colored cubic style being thrown up in every American city with a bloating population of young professionals. Even down the traditional looking rest of the street, the lights and tight congestion mirrored the other cities he had been to. It was a regressive kind of familiarity. Hands in his pockets, shoulders aggressively out, and with bored squinted eyes, he walked with the group to the subway. She was walking in front of him with Angela. His eyes were drawn to her dark coat. She had bought it the weekend before and had been excited to wear it around Madrid. She also wore a black beret, matching color jeans, and high boots. To him at least, she stood out in the crowd and city. And if it was just to him he didn't care. The coat was helping her walk confidently enough to mask her shyness and appear like these city girls. He was happy wear that mask comfortably. It was something she always had to do. Even around their little town. Her height made it easier, being almost as tall as him. It intimidated a lot of men to be eye to eye with her. He wasn't. He liked how it lined their vision together, where she would happily soften for him in their private space.

It was a short walk to the subway. When they got off there were multiple choices for places to go and the group seemed to know where they wanted to, so he followed. The bar was crowded. They weren't the only Americans there and the bar catered to that with the music. She was doing shots. He was too, but only with her. He didn't feel like being part of the big celebration an evening out was to this group. It was hard to move.

The people packing into the small space pushed her against him. They stared at each other while adjusting to the darkness. When he could see her, his eyes drifted down to her lips. The lipstick she was wearing matched her coat. In the dark bar the facelessness of the people made them feel alone and she kissed him. When they separated, Angela gave them each another shot and they took it. She put her face on his shoulder and thinking it was affection he hugged her, but she lifted her head a moment later and whispered loudly in his ear, "I'm seeing two of you."

Without saying anything, he took one of her hands and pushed his way out of the bar, hailed a taxi, and they got in.

"How are you feeling?" He asked, after giving the driver the address.

She just shook her head.

He kept holding her hand as the taxi drove down the dark unfamiliar road.

"I'm sorry." She said, after some silence.

"Don't apologize," He assured her, smiling and then looking out the window. "I don't care."

He saw her nod in his peripheral and they were silent a moment.

"Are you excited about your book?" She asked.

He paused and looked back at her. He had recently signed a publishing contract.

"Yeah, of course." He replied, squeezing her hand.

She looked down at the hand he had squeezed, then at him before looking out her window and moaning softly. "You still love her."

He blinked. His book was about another woman. One from what was a long time ago now. The driver hadn't reacted. He probably only knew a little English. Still, those were simple words and her tone was universal.

"I don't." He replied.

"No," She said, more drunkenly. "You love her. You'll always love her. That's why you wrote a book about her."

He didn't love this other woman anymore.

"I really don't." It was all he could say.

"No," She said, her voice getting shakier, "You still love her."

It was an insistence made crueler by the ineffectiveness of his denials, but it was too soon to tell her why.

Thankfully, the taxi had arrived in front of their hotel. He paid, then helped her out. She was mumbling incoherently. Holding her steady, they walked into the lobby and then got to their room quickly, but clumsily.

He put her to bed and got in expecting a cold reception. Instead she hugged him very tight. That's how they slept. Interrupted only by occasional trips made to the bathroom.

She was still sick in the morning. It was the afternoon by the time her vomiting had subsided enough to shower and eat the bread and water he had gotten her from a store on the corner.

"This is the most hungover I think I've ever been." She said as she got back under the covers.

"What do you think did it?" He was sitting by her feet and rubbing her legs lightly through the blankets.

"Those shots in the apartment were really sugary." She grumbled. "I wasn't thinking."

"The shots at the bar were tequila too."

"They were." She realized. "How were the rest of those girls downing them?"

"They're younger than we are." He said, laying down on top of the covers next to her.

"Are you saying I'm old?"

"No,"

"Yes you are. You're not hungover."

"One, I am a little. Two, I didn't drink as much as you. So if anything, I'm subtly saying I'm more mature."

She groaned and rolled over as if that made him go away.

He laughed and patted the bump her butt was making in the blankets, "I'm a little bigger than you too."

"Whatever," She said, still pretending to be angry. They were quiet for a minute. He went back to rubbing her legs, occasionally giving her calfs a squeeze.

"I don't think I can go out today." She said, softly into her hands wrapped up in the blanket covering her face.

"I thought so." He said.

"So you should go without me."

"You're sick. What if you need something?"

"I'll manage." She said, rolling over again. "Go, I don't want to keep you."

"I'll just wait for you to feel better."

"You're wasting your time in Madrid."

He didn't see it that way. "Madrid isn't going anywhere."

"You're going to make me feel bad about keeping you here instead of seeing the city."

"You shouldn't. You're sick and I'm worried about you. So I'll stay here and wait for you to feel better. Then we'll see Madrid together."

"Okay," She said, after a little pause.

"What do you want to do in the meantime?"

"That's the thing. I want to sleep. You should go out while I'm asleep."

"You won't be asleep very long." He said as he sat up and reached into his bag to grab his book. "I'll just read while you do and we'll see how you feel when you wake up."

She said okay again and was sleeping a moment later. He put his back against the wall and read his book peacefully.

He had dozed off a little while reading so he didn't know how much time had past when she stirred awake. She rolled over towards him and he put his book down to look at her.

"How are you feeling?" He asked.

"A little better." She replied. Only her eyes were peering out at him from under the covers. "Come here."

He lay down parallel to her, still on top of the blankets. Kissing her forehand, he put his arm over her.

"Come under," She said.

He tucked in his legs and got under with her. They hugged properly and he kissed the side of her head.

"Thank you for staying." She said.

"You like seeing me when you wake up?"

"Yes,"

"Do you think you can get up soon?"

"I can't. I still feel really nauseous." She put her face in his chest. "I'm sorry. Now more of the day is gone."

"It's still okay," He said and squeezed her gently.

"Thank you," She said, lifting her head up. Then he kissed her. They kissed for a long time. He started to undress her and she helped him. When they were naked under the covers he shifted on top of her.

"Slowly," She said, putting her arms over his neck and kissing him again.

He nodded.

After, she shifted so her face would be in his chest again and she could escape into him while hiding from the world under the blanket.

"I'm hungry." She said, after some time.

"What food do you want?" He asked.

"Pizza."

"In Spain?"

"There isn't a better hangover food."

"Okay," he said as he separated from her.

He got out of bed and started putting his clothes back on.

"Are you going to go get it."

"Yeah…" He said as he googled pizza on his phone. "How else would we get it?"

"Thank you,"

"There's a place like ten minutes away." He said putting his phone in his pocket and bending down to kiss her. "I'll be back in probably like a half-hour."

"You've been really sweet today."

"You're sick."

"It's my fault I'm sick." She said, embarrassed.

"I don't care." He replied, matter of factly.

Outside, he followed his phone to the pizza. It was early evening. Activity on the street was low enough to let him think about the day. He got to the pizza place and ordered. Then he walked back briskly so it would still be somewhat warm when she ate it.

"Thank you," She said, again. The repetitious sound of the phrase was starting to make her uncomfortable.

He sat down on the bed next to her and picked up a slice of his own.

"Can you eat this?" He asked, before taking a bite.

She nodded while chewing then said through a full mouth, "I'm not nauseous anymore."

"Good," He said as she swallowed.

"Do you want to take a walk after this?" She asked. "I know it's only one of the things we wanted to do but we could still go to the garden."

"I'd like that." He said, holding her hand as they continued to eat.

They left the hotel after they finished the pizza. It was becoming dark. The cool air tasted fresh. He looked at her walking next to him and smiled. They went a block down the street and then crossed the circular cobble plaza. On the other side was a paved path leading into the garden introduced by an arch decorated in Christmas lights. Beyond it were stands selling gifts and treats. They walked along the middle of the road, stopping and veering towards the stands that caught her eye. He had his elbow pointed outward so she could wrap her arms around him and let her body use his for support while they walked.

"This is nice." He said.

"It is. I'm sorry the whole day couldn't be like this."

"Stop apologizing, it happens."

"Even if it does, you could've been annoyed. Why weren't you?"

"I wanted to take care of you."

"You didn't have to."

"Well, I wanted to spend the day with you too."

"More than explore an amazing city?"

"Yeah,"

"Why?"

He walked with her in silence for a moment. Only a day had passed. It was still just as soon to say why.

"C'mon," She said. "How come?"

He didn't know what else to tell her.

"Hey," She said, stopping, "What is it? Are you okay?"

He smiled and nodded. He could tell her later.

Knowing his way around town now armed with a few practiced phrases. Ryan could now believe he was here. His friend owned a bar and that was a good place to practice. They had met when Ryan had heard music from his childhood playing outside and went in to see what sort of place did that. Then the two had become friends.

New Suits

The bar Peter had taken him to was small and dark with the exception of the bar-top itself, which was very bright from the dangling tiki lights above them. It was relatively early so they were the only two sitting at the bar, making the other groups around the tables almost invisible unless they turned around and really focused.

Greg's index finger played with the small plastic menu while his other hand held his can of beer. He had wanted a cocktail. The bar had a good selection specials, but Peter had warned him about the metal this country used to either dilute or preserve the alcohol. He couldn't remember. Regardless, it was off his menu despite the price. The beer was cheap enough. Everything was in this country despite it being the other world power. So his attraction to a cocktail had more to do with how much he would've liked to see himself with a drink as opposed to a beer.

"Yeah, I sometimes come here after class." Peter said. "It's actually more active on the weekdays than Friday or Saturday. The crowd is sort of different too. More social, especially to Americans, still a good place to start the night off."

Greg nodded at his friend. "It is. It's like casual but clean and cool. So we're not out of place or overdressed, more like making statement." The statement he was referring to was their suits.

On the first day of his visit Peter had taken him to a tailor downtown and for about $50 nice elderly ladies had measured him and had a suit and jacket ready earlier today. It was the first suit he had ever worn and it was his own that he had bought.

"So will your classes next semester be classes in Mandarin again?" He asked Peter.

Peter nodded and downed his beer. "Yeah, just one class this semester. Last one was two. I'll take some courses about Eastern stocks and comparative marketing techniques between the United States and China, should be cool."

"That'll be an interesting comparison."

"Yeah, course starts in like the 1950's and works its way up to now."

"That'll be crazy to see it pick up."

Peter nodded. "The difference in just a few years too. It's just such an economic powerhouse now."

"They got the American Dream." Greg said, sarcastically.

"They kinda do though." Peter said, slowly. "The grit of their workers, we could learn a lot from it. They work so much. And sometimes just rent little hotel rooms and sleep for an hour then get back to work. It's crazy. A lot of them don't even make that much money in the end, but they hustle."

Greg nodded and didn't say anything.

"There's a cultural course too." Peter continued. "It like gives you some understanding of their culture and its roots."

"This is an interesting culture." Greg said, dryly.

"Yeah, you're supposed to take this class first semester, but my schedule got messed up."

Greg nodded again. "Man, you were so smart for getting out here. And for studying Chinese when we were in high school, Sam too. It's going to give you such a leg up when we finish up with college."

"We'll see." Peter said. "You want another beer?"

"Yeah, wait a minute." Greg gulped the rest of his beer and slammed it down."

Peter grinned and raised his hand to get the bartender's attention. His big silver watch dropped down his wrist making a heavy clang when its descent was stopped by his widening forearm. It was a nice watch. He'd have to get one like it. It would be a good way to customize his suit to really give him an image. There were other things he could get, like cufflinks, that would help present him. He had never worn cufflinks but something about them seemed successful. A better beard could help on the self-presentation side. He brushed a hand over the thin cover of hair his face had produced over the last two weeks. If he was going to try and portray an image of what he wanted, he couldn't do it halfway.

When Peter got the bartender's attention, he ordered two more beers in what sounded to Greg like rapid gibberish. Peter had a similar scruff as him. It was more popular here.

"So what kind of place are we going to tonight?"

"Propaganda," Peter answered, "You'd like it. It's like a twenty minute cab from here in a tall building downtown. You go in an elevator up like twenty floors and the doors open and you're just in the club. It's wicked awesome."

"What time do we need to get there?"

Peter looked at his phone. "Kuo and Mike said they'd be there a little after midnight. I'll message Kuo when we leave."

"So we'll just get right in?"

"Yeah, they bought a table and we're on their list."

Greg nodded at Peter and took a drink from his beer. "That'll be pretty cool."

"Don't mention it to them though. They think it's normal, fucking Hong Kong."

"Yeah," Greg mumbled. "It's awesome you met them in your program. They seem cool." Then he grinned and said, snidely. "It also must be nice having all that money."

Peter laughed, "Yeah, they don't know anything else. They were the ones who told me about the tailor."

"Oh?" Greg replied, perking up. "They go there too?"

Peter shook his head. "No, they get their suits from somewhere in Europe, maybe Italy or something. They just knew about it and that I would want them cheap."

"Oh,"

"Yeah," Peter said, laughing again. "They're high end. We're not there yet. We have to scheme a little to look nice."

"Yeah," Greg replied, more softly this time.

"It's better that way though, dude." Peter said, putting both palms on the top of the bar and pushing down on nothing. "With our way we have to build something. So when we have money to spend like them we'll appreciate it."

Greg inhaled and tried to bring his excitement up.

"You get what I'm saying?" Peter asked, aggressively shaking Greg's shoulder and thumping his chest rhythmically with his closed other hand.

"Fucking right," He agreed with Peter. "It'll be ours. Something we made. That's something they can't have because it was never on the line for them. That's why I have to get out here and focus on working and learning the language. Fuck, I'll start with Rosetta Stone once I'm back home to build a foundation ready for when I come back. There's so much to put on your resume here and after a few years hustling, then I'll be able to come home, wicked qualified."

"Exactly, get out here dude," Peter said, jabbing the table with his pointer finger. "Get out here, I'm not going anywhere.

You know once I'm done with studying abroad it's only one year back at school before I'm right back here. We'll live together and work on making something together. They squeeze you out just like New York would but the living is cheaper and you said it, we come back bi-lingual and more qualified as long as we've got our eye on the ball and we're always closing shit. Then we're back, successful, and get to start living, guaranteed."

"Yeah, man, guaranteed." Greg said to his friend. "With our own success we made ourselves. It's important"

"We don't have a choice." Peter said.

"No," Greg said, now imagining the work and risk that was starting to wane his excitement in what they were excitedly prophesying. "No, we don't."

Peter ordered another two beers even though neither of them had finished. Meanwhile, Greg turned around to look at the others. The men at the tables were dressed like they were and the women in the way their gender could personalize the uniform. They all wanted the same thing as he and his friend. So did most of the people in the apartments above the bar and all along the tightly packed street of tall buildings. On this street alone there were thousands of competitors, some had to be harder working, others smarter, shrewder, or just more cut-throat. Then on the next street were the same people with different faces and the same with the next one. In the homes and offices around him, the competition ballooned to the ten thousands, hundreds of thousands, and then millions, which then went even higher when considering whole cities at a time and even further so when cities lumped together into countries. Even if Greg had the real number it was unfathomable. And here, focused back down to Greg and his friend, were their vague plans and their new suits. Every person had said what he had said and heard what Peter had. How could they not when the goal was always the same when the goal of their business is the natural reward of a successful one? They'd all vie for the same few select spots, most of which would be occupied by ones born into it. Then once it was clear what they wanted wouldn't happen they'd have to try again and again, endlessly clamoring for enough luck to let them into the world they wanted, always just out of reach enough to be stupid.

It was getting darker. Summer was over, which meant that Ryan had lived a whole season here. The air still felt like summer but the leaves were turning and falling. Ryan was finding the leaves lackluster. His standards had been shaped by his home to be higher than he had ever realized. He also hadn't realized how much he would miss his more colorful autumn.

No Words

The sun had been shining through the blinds for a long time. The rays had at first been the usual reminder that he should be awake. However, aware she had been much quicker to do the same, he had been able to just close his eyes and drift back into a heavy trance that felt fine to linger in.

Now, awake again and knowing he wouldn't fall back asleep, he fought his lethargy by pulling off the blankets. The chill of the room stung his naked body, giving him more than enough reason to sit up. She either felt some of the cold or had been relying on his heat because she rolled away to tighten the blanket around her. Smiling, he rotated his body and stretched his legs off the futon. Ignoring the second shiver as his heels touched the floor, he pointed his toes up and felt his blood flow through his lower body. It gave him the motivation to get up and walk through the main area to the bathroom in the hallway, where he relieved himself and walked out into what was now a much warmer apartment.

The cocoon she had rolled the blanket into had unfurled and her feet were sticking out while her hands were rubbing each half of her face. A motion that had pushed the blankets below her bare chest. Staring for a moment, he felt a simple comfort along with his attraction to her.

She took her hands off her face as she felt his weight. Smiling down while he sat on her, he picked up his phone to type into the translator, *"I'm sorry, I didn't mean to wake you up."*

Showing her his phone, she squinted a moment then replied, "No, is okey." She took the device and typed her own message that read, *"It is late. We should wake up now anyway."*

He nodded and took his phone back, tossing it down next to the futon. She moved her hips to ask if he was getting off. Pursing his lips and looking away, he shrugged his shoulders. She smiled upwards and squeezed the tops of his legs. Her eyes were open to him. They were a misty blue like the ocean on a cold dark day in winter, which to a water-child like him, created a dilemma like the delicate purity of untouched fallen snow. But she wasn't delicate, having the strength and beautiful firmness that could be expected from a ballerina. The muscle in her shoulders and arms were lean and defined and he could count her abdominals regardless if she was flexing her stomach or not.

He bent down, bringing his face close to hers, holding himself up with his elbows. She didn't need him to say anything. Gradually bringing himself down onto her, he placed one hand under her back and put the other through her golden hair as they kissed.

When they stopped, he picked his phone back up and translated another message.

"I'm going to take a shower."

"Okey." She replied, putting a hand through his hair now. "Duchas. I cook now. Then I go."

He nodded and gave her a peck on the lips before gathering his clothes and going back to the bathroom.

The hot water from the shower immediately washed away the grime and dried sweat from the previous night and he came out of the bathroom dressed in his simple jeans and t-shirt. Once he was a few feet away from the smell of soaps permeating in the bathroom, breakfast started drifting into his nostrils. He entered the main area and saw her in front of the stove on the left wall, cooking in only her revealing underwear bottoms.

"You like the food?" She asked, giggling from the kisses on the back of her neck.

He put his chin on her shoulder and looked down at what she was making. It was a simple breakfast of eggs, toast, and orange juice.

"It looks great." He said.

"Great!" She asked.

He nodded, "Great."

"Thank you, baby." She said, putting the spatula down so she could turn around and kiss him again.

"I shower now." She said after they parted, then picked up her phone to write the message. *"You can eat. I will be a while because I have to put on make up and wash my hair."*

He read the message then took her phone, *"It's okay. I'll wait for you to eat. Take your time."*

She read the translation and shook her head. *"No, I will take a long time. I made this food for you. I was eating small things while you showered."*

"Bien," He said, trying to be more like her.

"No escuchaste mi guapo," She said, coyly. She knew he could understand the essence but not the words. "Dije la comida fue para ti."

He laughed and shrugged his shoulders, repeating, "Bien," with a smile.

"Si," She said, slowly. "Is okey." Then she broke from the hug, picking up the plates and glass, to slowly and deliberately walk to the other side of the room where the table was.

He watched her walk. Then went over himself as she set everything down.

"Okey baby." She said, touching his cheek as she walked by him. "I shower now. You eat now."

He squeezed her hand affectionately before she was too far away. "Para ti," She said, nodding at the food. He had figured out the meaning of that one.

Again he watched her walk away, still awestruck despite the time the two of them had spent together. He sat down to eat. The food tasted better than he knew it really was. After, he washed and stacked the dishes. Then made the futon to kill more time. When the futon looked as good as he could make it, he lay down and sent messages to his friends. They were interested in her. He had posted pictures of them together last weekend when they had gone to the Old Capital. It had been a good trip. People had thought they were both Americans and she had gotten shy when they had spoken to her in English.

Her timidity around people making that incorrect assumption was funny since she was usually very confident. He had been more so than usual when they met. Or maybe it had been apathy manifesting in the isolation of living alone in a place where he couldn't speak the language only masquerading as confidence.

"Hola baby," She said when she walked back into the bedroom wearing loud pink pants and a black mesh half-shirt of a foreign brand he didn't recognize. She took out her phone and asked, "*What do you want to do today?*"

He typed his own message, "*I still haven't seen your local shrine. Isn't it near the beach too?*"

"*Yes, but it's very far.*"

"*You don't like walking around with me?*"

"No, no true." She said, hitting him on the chest playfully. *"Okay, we can go to the bus now."*

Her apartment building was on top of a hill. The company provided it so her co-workers also lived there. They waved to the ones who were smoking over the hallway's thick concrete balcony and to the others loitering by their cars in front of the building. Walking down the hill through the hot air gave them a view of the town that seemed hazy through the humidity and bright sun. Rice paddies were directly below where the ground leveled out and along either side of them were two story houses with triangular roofs styled with crossing ridges, numerous enough to make them look like the houses had goose bumps. At the edge of the rice paddies was a man-made river and beyond that were more houses, interrupted only by the flat smooth tops of shops and the station towering over the rest of the town.

They stopped on the narrow bridge while crossing the river. It looked thin and shallow, only taking up about half the space that had been dug out for it. Despite that, the water utilized what it had and moved rapidly along the cement bank.

"Look, is a date!" She said, excitedly, pointing at two ducks sitting side by side on the edge of the water, immobile and looking straight forward. He looked at them too.

"Is a date." She said again, chuckling a little. He looked at her with a plain smile and nodded.

She smiled back more genuinely and tugged on his arm. "Come on everybody." Making a joke at the direct translation of one of her language's more common phrases. They kept going across the bridge and through the maze of town, nodding at the polite residents until they got to the station.

The building itself was only two stories, but the high ceilings gave it its formidable size for the town. There were stops for local busses and a small parking lot in front of the station. Between the station and the lot was a half circle, lined with glass stands above benches where they could wait for the bus.

They sat on their bench, playing flirtatious games with each other while they waited, ignoring the more polite and formal residents on other benches. When their moss green bus arrived, they got on and walked to the back so they could upgraded their flirting to kissing.

It wasn't a long ride. They got off a stop before the last at the shrine, which was placed neatly on top of a hill encircled by a knee-high old fence. At the entrance were two small fox statues made of pale weathered stone. They walked up the hill surrounded by surprisingly dense foliage and stopped at the foot of the shrine. It was only about five feet tall and was a chest with an open face only covered by thin bamboo sticks. Four fatter sticks of bamboo were stuck into each corner of the chest propping up a moss covered roof with the same aesthetic as the roofs of the homes they had seen.

There was an aesthetic nobility to the little old shrine. Its permanence bothered the young lovers, but they examined it quietly to respectfully absorb the culture of their shared guest country. The trees around them seem to thicken and the familiar sounds that came into the sacred space from the outside made them feel intrusive and alien.

After scanning the shrine a quick second time for peace of mind, he put his fingers through the spaces between hers. She looked at him and he tilted his head in the direction exiting the shrine. She squeezed his hand tighter and hugged him with her other arm. They walked out together holding each other's fingers hooked by the small knuckle. Once outside of the small contained forest, they kissed passionately and started walking in the direction of the distant sound of waves.

The landscape changed abruptly to a sandy off-road desert with the satisfying taste of salt in the air and sound of gulls. The dunes were a small wall they relinquished their hold on each other to climb, which then became a messy hill to roll playfully down together. The beach was empty and wasn't particularly nice. They were unaware though. After rolling down to the bottom like children, they lay in the sand. He was under her. She was resting her head on his chest and had her eyes closed. As the hot sand began to cool, he put the tips of his fingers on her skin and massaged her. After a few minutes, he patted her back for attention. She looked down at him and raised an eyebrow. He pointed at the water with both hands. Understanding what he wanted, she stood up and took her shirt off, which she threw in his face. He laughed and got up before taking the piece of clothing off him. When he did, he saw she was already in her underwear, standing in front of him with one hip out and hands over both of them. She smiled, amused, while she waited for him to get undressed. When he had, she felt his arms and placed a hand on his stomach that had been burned away and hardened throughout his year in this country of healthier food. Thinking she wanted another kiss, he bent forward, but she took off towards the water. He watched her run for a second. Then went after her, leaving their clothes unattended in the sand of this nearly crime-less country.

It was low tide. She ran over the knee high waves and dived into the warm water once it was deep enough. Close behind, he jumped off the edge of the undertow in a much less dignified way. When he resurfaced, she was waiting for him, treading water. Latching her limbs down on him like a clamp, the two sank. Underwater, they opened their eyes together and saw each other. She kissed him flat and hard then kicked off him, propelling to the surface. He followed. This time she only wrapped her legs around him, keeping her head above by moving her arms beneath the surface. He put his arms on her behind under the water and kicked his legs. She rolled her eyes and together they kept one another afloat while indulging their attraction to one another. When they had had enough, they sat on the shore and looked at the water.

His home was in that direction. As his eyes adjusted and his vision spanned further out over the miles of sea he felt closer to it. She had her head resting on his shoulder. He wondered if she was thinking of her home too. It was technically that way too. But it wasn't the same. The ocean was just calming and beautiful.

The small waves were hitting the sand a few feet in front of them, then expanding across the shore, sometimes reaching their toes.

"They're getting stronger though." He thought. "The tide is coming in and we'll have to move soon."

But they stayed put in happy silence watching the ocean as the brightness of midday darkened into regular afternoon. It still wasn't cold. When the waves started to hit their shins he again decided it was time to leave and he turned his body onto her for a last kiss to end their date. She collapsed, covering herself with his body as they kissed more passionately.

A wave passed over them, which broke their affection with laughter.

"I wonder if she knows what *From Here to Eternity* is?" He thought. "Or even if she's seen the scene on a classic reel montage?"

It didn't matter.

They dried off and went home feeling tired all over again. This time showering together and collapsing on the covers of her futon, naked, and then falling asleep.

It was dark when he woke up. He was on his side facing away from her. She was rubbing a hand lightly on his exposed waist. Rolling over towards her with his eyes still closed, he pushed his face in her chest. She kissed the top of his head, saying something sounding sweet, but sad. Words he couldn't understand. There was a lot he wished he could say to her. He didn't bother to reach for his phone to try. Even if that thing could say what he wanted, it was best he didn't because it didn't have to be said. That went for what was good and what wasn't. Her words continued and her voice was getting slower and more resolved. He liked to listen to her. Beyond her accent, universally tantalizing to men of his country, there was a happy sweetness that gave everything she said a happier existence once out of her mouth and into his world. So he wished he hadn't understood her saddest two words standing out among the tangled other dozens that linked in his ears like a single intermingled sound. He wished for the first time since he had met her, his ignorance had actually been greater so he didn't have to hear those words stand out in her private confession. She also knew it was over. That as comforting as their attraction with no words could be, it was still only a stand in created by lonely circumstance, made more alluring to them because it alleviated the symptoms the circumstance created. It couldn't be more. Already they had gone too far and accidentally made it worse. So he clamped his already closed eyes shut even more and hugged her tightly one last time.

Ryan was calling his friends and family more often now. He knew he hadn't been gone for very long. Still, he found himself creating a dichotomy between his life in America and here.

Meaning

Brandon was in bed already, watching a show he didn't care about on his computer. He paused the show and searched for alternative entertainment before closing the device. Laying down with his head in his pillow gave him temporary relief. While it lasted, Brandon felt his legs and arms tingle and then freeze like he had become a statue. He closed his eyes to complete the spell, but that only broke it. His body regained its feeling and since he couldn't see any point in trying anymore, he turned the light on and got out of bed.

He didn't need to go to sleep anyway. It had been a productive day off so there was nothing pressing tomorrow. In the sense that he didn't have much energy, he was tired. But since he couldn't sleep, he might as well do something.

Getting dressed, Brandon thought of what that could be. His options weren't great since there wasn't anyone he particularly wanted to call. There was always the pub that he walked by on the way home from work. That could be a low-key way to kill time. It was still early enough for the night-owl youths to be getting ready for their late night out Brandon had no interest in. Hopefully by the time they were emerging he would be ready for bed.

Selecting a standard outfit of a t-shirt, flannel, and shoes, Brandon stood dressed in the middle of his studio-apartment awkwardly. He had a few other things to wear but they weren't better or worse. After going into the bathroom to brush his teeth and mat his hair, he was ready. With nothing else keeping him from going out, he put his phone, wallet, and keys in his pockets and left.

The night was a cool one. It was dark even under the lamp-light. There was a cold wind too, but not enough to disperse the mist. Brandon, hands in his pockets, walked down the old fashioned cobbled streets along the rows of tight homes he had more associated with a fairy-tale growing up than a real place to live. Now they were homes like his own. Expensive, downtown homes with plenty of modernity inside. Still, they had been charming enough for Brandon to rent when he had arrived, even if they had been slightly above his means. Now years later when he didn't need to tighten his belt, Brandon felt a calling to the new cheaper apartments outside the old city that would make his screen better mirror his friends' back home when they spoke online.

Brandon took the right down the smaller, darker, quieter, version of the main street, where his intended pub was. It was a good looking place. Celtic in that had a dankness to it even though it was well lit. Brandon couldn't place why he was drawn here. Maybe he wasn't and that was why he hadn't gone in after all these years. It was just *his* foreign neighborhood pub by default proximity.

He sat down at the half empty wooden bar with linoleum covering. He had chosen a seat where nobody was next to him. The pub was small inside, where a narrow walkway separated the barstools from the wall, which opened into a space for three small tables when the bar ended. The wall was decorated with Gaelic crests, pictures of rugby teams, and the highlands. In the middle of the decorations was a single unisex bathroom where the white silhouette was wearing a kilt. Brandon ordered an American beer and sipped it slowly, using his index finger to play with his napkin while he tried to think how the thoughts going through his mind could be used for work. But it wasn't the happy, grateful, American guest they wanted from him.

The beer didn't taste right. He had to drink half of it to be sure. But he had visited home not too long ago and it definitely wasn't right. He drank the rest quickly and ordered an ale.

"What's with your face?" A slurred voice said into his ear.

Brandon pulled his head back to see a woman his age being handed a whiskey soda. She gave the bartender her card and looked back at Brandon for his answer.

"What do you mean?" Brandon asked. "I can't help my face I'm pretty sure." He ended his sentence with the intonation of a question and a raised eyebrow. His words were hollow coming up his throat before practice sugar-coated them.

The young woman smiled and sipped the drink from her straw. She was pretty. Not especially beautiful in the tired mainstream sense. There was a playful, almost boyish nature that Brandon could pick up on. It reminded him of the girls he had grown up with. Her hair was the red Brandon had expected to be more common here, same with her freckles and green eyes. While he examined her a dangerous extra second, Brandon decided this woman would look best standing in one of this country's valleys or meadows when it was still wet from rain. Exemplifying the reward understood by the people who lived in this less than popular climate.

"You don't look that happy." She said, after she took a sip from the straw. "Somebody hurt yah, hon?"

Brandon shrugged and replied, "Not really, I mean, are you asking like ever? Yeah, but I don't think that's what's up with my face."

The young woman pursed her lips and nodded as the bartender gave her back her card and the receipt which she signed and returned.

"So then what's the problem." She asked.

"I don't think there is one." Brandon lied. He was trying to let her help make that true.

"Just thinking deep thoughts then?" She asked.

"Something like that." Brandon said, smiling. "Do you want to sit down?" Motioning to the empty seat her thin body was hovering over.

She looked up at the ceiling and shifted her mouth to the side pretending to consider it. "Okay," She answered. "But if those girls in the back are giving skeptical eyes it's only because my friends are also my bodyguards."

Brandon looked to the back of the bar without moving his head. He picked out the table with her three friends. They were all staring with grins that would easily fold into giggles. Brandon looked back at the young woman. She had already sat down, her elbow close to his arm on the bar, which helped her palm prop up her face flirtatiously close to his.

"Why do you need bodyguards?" Brandon asked.

"In case you get a little too excited."

"Do I look like the type?"

"You're a man aren't you?"

"That's a little general." Brandon replied, glibly.

She rolled her eyes. "Maybe, but I still might need a little backup."

"You don't look like a wuss."

"A wuss?" She said and laughed. "I mean that maybe... I haven't been at this in awhile..."

"So you were projecting little when you asked if someone hurt me."

She shrugged.

"Is that why you talked to me?" Brandon asked.

She shrugged again, "Maybe a little, doesn't mean you're not cute."

Brandon looked into this young woman's eyes again. The more he talked to her the less the words coming out of his mouth needed to hide.

"So you're American?" She asked, the other shoe dropping.

Brandon paused. He swallowed and answered that he was. That started the predictable series of questions, which then pressured him to ask questions that were equally bland. It wasn't her fault. He had been living here long enough to find this tiring. She hadn't been spending that time around foreigners. So while he would stick out to her, she'd become more and more like the dozens if not hundreds of faces he had had this conversation with. That's what he always would be here. Even if he lived the rest of his life in this country, the first thing people would always ask would be if he was here on *holiday* and after it was established he wasn't, another array of inevitability was ready for him.

Meeting this woman had become stale. But Brandon learned her name, her interests, her job, her dreams, and her number. After that, he felt comfortable making the excuse to leave. An excuse she found refreshingly gentlemanly. She kissed him to her friends' excitement. The kiss landed and made her happy. Brandon told her goodbye and left.

Outside, he turned towards home. It had gotten only marginally colder, but Brandon was shivering. Still, when he came to his apartment he kept walking. He knew he wasn't ready to sleep. The first night-owls were emerging. Brandon's opinion of them had little to do with their age. They were only a little younger than him. But they were enjoying his life's previous chapter. The one he associated with his arrival to this country, city, and neighborhood. So to him, they were children. Ignorant of the complications and pressures he felt from their strung-out euphoria given by early adulthood's burst of freedom.

He reached the top of the road. Sitting in front of the local castle, he looked out at the city. The mist had gotten thicker, but familiarity made out the different landmarks. He didn't try to recapture how he felt his first time looking out at this city. It had been a morning clearer and brighter than usual. It would have been a day beautiful to him no matter what from the high of newness, much like the night-owls he had passed on his way up here. He had built a life in this country, but he hadn't laid down roots. He wasn't able. He knew some like him who had, but it hadn't worked for him. He had never gotten past always being different and everyone seeing him as so. Now his skill-set predicated on being different by definition, creating an advantage that was hard to walk away from. The whole reason he had come here, after the prospect of simple adventure, had been to avoid being trapped like his friends who had felt they were staring down the barrel of a pointless life as they fulfilled each predictable milestone. But he was trapped too. He did his job as someone with a different perspective. One that would always excite the people here, like the young woman tonight at the pub. Back home he was the same and would have to start his life over again, working without his accustomed advantage. So he was trapped in the same room with only the saving grace of a different design and outside view.

So what had been the point? Brandon wanted to growl. He hugged himself closer. There hadn't been one. He was who he was. The enjoyable perks of new exposure wore off fast and even if he grew there were always costs. You couldn't cheat or run away until it was over because the result was the same. Whether he was here or at a place he called home. Life's finite trudge would continue and his empty feeling made the approaching end more terrifying. He needed fulfillment that was deeper than intoxicating himself with a unique path and new places. He had to have meaning.

Ryan was homesick now. The difficulty of doing everyday activities in a foreign language had lost its charm and were only annoying now. He found himself constantly comparing his culture to where he was and more often than not his won. Ryan wanted to go home.

Cherry Blossom Viewing

Ryan Clarke was twenty-three years old.

The Hanami is a festival that celebrates renewal. It's held in the early days of Spring which is decided when the buds covering the usually pale barren branches bloom with pink sakura. The festival is one families and groups of friends plan alone, but do around each other in whatever part of their city or town the flowers are best enjoyed. Sakura flowers are fragile and their time in bloom is fleeting. Making the first signs of life's end equally prevalent during this celebration of beginning. The petals fall among the picnic like snowflakes from the shade above. This is not shade from harsh sun or rain but from acknowledgment of the trials that will inevitably corrupt life's newborn beauty so one can instead indulge in its potential.

Ryan wasn't speaking to anyone. He wasn't angry or being anti-social and neither were his friends talking around him. It was just something that sometimes happened when second-languages are the only means of communication.

Being excluded from the passionate but apparently funny conversation allowed Ryan to take in the bright fullness above him a second time without the pressures and influences of group observation. The swaying of the branches was comforting to him. He hadn't been able to see it at first but focus had revealed a slight sway. It made the falling petals seem less like the regulated sand of an hourglass and more free. Like they fell when they believed the ground was ready to be infused and revitalized with the addition of their warm color after being cold and barren all winter.

It had not been a bad winter. Warm for Ryan's standards, but somehow hollow from a lack of snow. This spring was gratifying though. He was happy he was here.

The castle could be narrowly seen through the foliage. It was a humble but firm castle. Painted black and white, built five hundred years ago to be a symbol of a prosperous time, recently restored to serve that image again.

But mostly it was just a local monument in the center of the city to people, so Ryan did his best to not fabricate meaning unto it. Instead he thought it was more important to look at the castle through the shade and remember where he was.

He would not be here forever. That was never really considered beyond a few days when this had all been brand new. Still, he'd be here for some time. Longer than average even after the bottom rung of those who don't last out the year were removed. There wasn't a hurry to leave whether that meant home or somewhere else.

Ryan brought his chin back down and looked over the group of locals who had become his friends. He was excited about his new life now that he had it.

Walking home from work, Ryan noticed the last of the pink petals had fallen. It would be a year until he saw them again. And he felt like he would.

Sandy Dunes

Jaime was tired of sitting on the bus. The desert and the high cliffs surrounding the road that had been exciting when they had first gotten an hour or so out of Meknes were now just scenery. Most of the others on the tour were sharing the same sentiment and those who weren't feeling travel fatigue were making it worse. He wasn't interested in the movie playing on the small screens along the bus's ceiling. He was tired of his music. And he couldn't sleep from the constant bumps in the road. His only option was to read, which he didn't consider a bad alternative but like the other distractions had worn out its appeal.

It was a lesser known book by John Hersey about a suburbanite who meets a local on Martha's Vineyard and gets taught wisdom through fishing. He would've preferred to be taking more time in between each lesson separated by chapter. But with this being the only viable option left to stave off frustrating boredom he was forced to consume large chunks of the small book at once. He had found it by accident at a street faire in Segovia the day before the trip. Recognizing the name of the author, he had picked up the book, and then seeing it took place off Martha's Vineyard made him homesick enough for his mid-cape town. Being a only casual fisher, what drew him were the passages about their boat and the sensations of being afloat. Because if he knew anything it was being on the sea. He had always been drawn to it, running in as a child, always swimming out further than he probably should've, and finally finding the proper channel for his need to head out onto open water in boats. Cleaning boats at ten, renting them at twelve, teaching sailing at thirteen, which eventually graduated to working with the tourists yachts at the club. But he wanted the ocean not the shore. So he became a merchant marine. The job had given him freedom and quenched his need to explore. So when he had finished, not knowing what to do now and at the time wanting to go home even less, he had gotten a job in England since Brighton had been a favorite stop of his. Despite being near the water, his new life was on land most days, many going by without him even seeing the water. Now as Jaime went deeper and deeper into the dry wasteland how much the ocean couldn't be replaced for him crystalized.

His friend Jasmin was sleeping next to him. She could always nap. Jaime envied how she could pass out and essentially teleport to their destination. Complaining was stupid though. They were going to sleep in a desert camp. It would've been pointless if they didn't go deep in the middle of sandy wasteland. Chastising himself for his impatience, Jaime went back to his book resolving he could always read it again properly.

At night, they got off the bus in a small town that besides their hotel was void of unnatural lighting. They dropped their bags off in the hotel's storage then went out the back to where a dozen jeeps were waiting for them. He crammed into the small car with Jasmin and the two other girls he was traveling with, Caroline and Kelly, then the driver took off. The desert flying by him was again interesting for a brief period that eventually settled into normalcy like the bus. The girls were having fun from the bumps and small jumps, laughing and cheering. It didn't quite live up to being on the ocean during rough weather but by the end Jaime had woken up a little from their energy.

When the jeep slowed, the girls calmed down and shout excitedly at what they were seeing. Laid out before them and the other jeeps that were lining up alongside them were hundreds of camels.

The strangeness of seeing animals he had seen hundreds of times only in photographs and on screens made Jaime pause. The girls started excitedly getting out of the jeep, reminding Jaime he could get closer to them. He got out and slowly walked towards the large animals with the conglomerating tour. Once he was closer, Jaime realized the camels were not in a random herd but loose lines that the Bedouins herding them were vigilantly maintaining. They were bigger than he had ever realized and smelled worse than horses with gobs of drool around their mouths that would get periodically dispelled by snorts.

Other members of the tour started getting hoisted up by the Bedouins. Jaime and his group waited for their turn while further taking in the animals.

A Bedouin approached them leading a camel with three attached by ropes behind it. Caroline bravely walked up to the leader and received an angry grunt, making her yell and jump back.

The Bedouin looked at him and Jaime shrugged and walked up to the camel. The camel looked into his eyes letting off another annoyed elongated grunt. He kept walking. Angry animals weren't going to scare him when his feet were on the ground more than the ones that had circled under him. The Bedouin tapped Jaime's shoulder and ushered him to the side of the animal, saying words he couldn't understand. Jaime put his foot in the stirrup like he had seen in movies and lifted himself up before he'd let the man help him.

The camel was rough. He shifted on the saddle realizing how tender his inner thighs were, triggering memories of looking down at his blistered palms after leaving work as a child. It was hard to look backwards but he could hear the girls getting on each camel and then they started moving forward. The movements felt rocky, where Jaime could feel the imbalance of the leg disconnected from the others in the air and then the brief the press and sink into the sand, making a brief new standard before another leg disrupted it again.

Jaime glanced upward at the stars. There were millions of them. A pleasant reminder of what he had been missing since moving to Brighton. It was something he had grown up looking at, so the concept wasn't new even if the constellations had moved on him but it was the first time in awhile he had looked up and felt something different. The camel began ascending a hill and he lowered his gaze when the steps leveled out again. The view shocked him. He was looking at miles of desert with nothing but dunes that as they gradually approached seemed to roll towards them like waves.

Each line of camels followed one another forming a long caravan moving down a road unseen to Jaime. The Bedouins walked alongside each group holding the reins of the lead camel like how Jaime's father had held onto the lines tight for him the first time they had been sailing.

"Oh my god, the stars." Caroline, said, noticing them as they reached the top of another dune where the sky seemed to press itself up to the rest of them, magnifying what was to them the foreign beauty of the natural world.

"Guys," Kelly said, "We're on camels in the Sahara desert right now."

Jaime smiled. It was nice.

Without any conception of how long the ride was, it ended at an assortment of yurts that appeared in the night.

Jaime jumped down off the camel before the Bedouin came to help him and wandered into the circular camp outlined by the yurts. There was a lit campfire in the middle of the camp. When Jaime reached the flames he was able to see the large dune looming over the camp. It wasn't a dune like his camel had traversed over. It was massive and made Jaime take an exhaustive sigh, knowing he'd have to get on top of it.

The camp was soon swarming with tour members exploring and picking yurts. The girls were calling Jaime over to the yurt they had chosen, so he walked over and lifted the heavy mat so he could bend down and walk in. The yurt's high ceiling gave more space than he had imagined from the outside. The air in the tent was warm and thick from a lack of circulation. The heat relaxed Jaime, which made him tired as the distance he had traveled that day weighed on his body. There were two rows of three mats made out of some kind of thick leather, meaning there was room for two more people in addition to their group. There seemed to be enough yurts to support each group's privacy though. Jaime put down his backpack that had his change of clothes on a bed and stretched his arms in the air with his finger's locked. Kelly was already laying on her bed, while Jasmin and Caroline riffled through their bags.

"My thighs' are going to be so sore tomorrow." Kelly said as she put her face in her bed's pillow.

"Yeah, and then you get back on the camel." Jasmin laughed as she pulled a comb from her bag and started brushing out the knots in her hair. "Besides, it was worth it."

"Yeah," Kelly replied, folding her arms on the pillow and resting her chin on it. "The desert and stars were so beautiful."

"Plus you rode a camel." Jasmin laughed.

"I sort of got over that." Kelly laughed back. "I was more into where we were than what we were doing."

Jamie shrugged when Kelly looked at him.

"Let's see what they're going to feed us." Caroline said. "I'm starving."

"I hope it isn't a camel." Jasmin said, her eyes getting wide.

"Oh shit, do you think they do that?" Caroline asked, also sounding worried.

"They have to eat something out here." Jasmin replied, showing all her teeth. "So why not?

"Yeah," Caroline said, pursing her lips and nodding, "Well we have to find out at some point, let's go."

Dinner was in the biggest yurt at the foot of the big dune. Like their yurt, the floor was covered in thick matting. In the center was a long table lined with pillows for them to sit cross-legged on. At each seat was a plate with a metal cover over its contents. Jaime lifted the cover by the thin handle and found a basic plate of chicken peas and rice with a weak alcohol made from grapes that the Bedouins got an exception for in this dry country.

After dinner, the group went around the fire and the nomads put on a show beating their drums. Intellectually, Jaime knew they were probably acting as opposed to this actually being a genuine cultural experience. But he still couldn't help have fun for awhile while the tour passed around various bottles of smuggled whiskey and vodka. Once the novelty of it was gone, he glanced up above the fire at the dune standing above them like it was just under the stars. He was on the sand now and felt the elements and life that came with that.

In the morning, Jaime woke up to Kelly's alarm screeching only a few hours after they had passed out. It was an hour before dawn and they were going up the dune together. The morning was still chilly but knowing the exertion of climbing kept them to wearing just sweaters. Their feet only had on socks since sand would turn whatever shoes they wore into weights. Jaime led his friends up the hill. His legs were soon burning and his hangover exacerbated the struggle. He had thought he had gone up dunes before. Now he realized the ones he had climbed growing up were not only smaller but packed by moister from the rain and sea. Sliding back down and slipping more than he ever had, he grabbed onto the sand for support and crawled like an animal up in the dark. After a while he turned around and saw the dark figures of his friends were doing the same thing. The sand was starting to brighten up. He was almost to the top and could hear the voices of the groups that had beaten them up there. Mustering up extra reserves of energy, Jaime propelled himself up and collapsed on his back across the long top of the dune, where he waited like that as the others caught up with him. When they were together, they sat close to alleviate their already falling body temperature. The sun started to rise across the desert. His friends gasped and Jaime grinned as he looked out at the ocean of gold in front of him, happy he had come.

Ryan was browsing a map on his computer. Every once in a while typing different cities into the directional key to see how long a way it was from his city. There was a lot in this country he hadn't seen yet.

Bottom of the World

He was here. This had to be here since there wasn't anything further south. It had been a long way. A plane to Texas, a plane to South America, a plane to the south of South America, then a bus to the last town in South America, and finally a bus to the park, before a boat took them across a huge lake to the first camp-site. Now they had stopped traveling, their journey about to begin.

Anthony's girlfriend Jessica was making sandwiches. It was almost lunchtime and after they ate they would get moving.

"You want chips on your sandwich, right?" She asked, not looking up.

Anthony replied he did. Looking at the mountains surrounding the trail.

"Okay, and you want it triple stacked too, right?"

"Yes, please," He said, absently, still looking as she made sandwiches on the picnic table. The number of mountains was overwhelming since each individual one reminded him of the mountains he had seen the few times he had gone skiing. They had always stood out in relation to everything around, being the biggest thing. These ones were all on top of each other, which made the world in front of him incredibly wide open and free at eye level but feel enclosed when looking up.

"Here you go." Jessica said, handing him a peanut butter and jelly sandwich. He looked at her as he took it, said thank you, and turned back at the mountains. Since he had been expecting more snow, the ice lining the mountain tops had taken his focus. It wasn't particularly cold down where they were. Anthony was even a little warm in his layers. The wind had been strong during the boat ride but it had disappeared after they had gotten off. He bit into his large sandwich, crunching through the potato chips.

Immediately before them was a meadow with a trail cutting through knee high grass that gradually turned into a valley between the bases of two mountains.

"How far is it to the glacier?" Jessica asked, finishing her own sandwich.

"Seven and a half kilometers," Anthony replied from memory. "I think that's like four miles."

"It doesn't sound too far does it?" Jessica laughed, looking up at the mountains like Anthony.

"No," Anthony agreed. "Not after how far we've come."

"It's uphill I guess." Jessica replied, not really listening.

"Half of it anyway." Anthony said, back, not feeling the need to correct her.

"Yeah, I can't believe we're even really here. You know?"

"What did you forget about all those planes and busses?" Anthony laughed.

She made a face at him. "No, I mean it's like this place isn't even real, like I can't be here because it's where other people go."

"It's a lot all at once."

"You sound like you're disappointed."

"I'm not." Anthony assured her. It was true, he was happy to be here.

They started on the trail a few minutes after their lunch. Anthony had taken off his coat and put it in his bag. It had been the right decision. He was already feeling beads of sweat form on his forehead as the meadow inclined. Soon their grassy dirt trail had hardened completely into rock. The two mountains moved in surprisingly quickly and then they were moving up a steep incline, needing their hands to steady themselves.

This first obstacle that involved movement out of the ordinary at first excited Anthony subconsciously. His legs started working with a springy energy that propelled him up faster than he realized. When a shout from Jessica stopped him, he looked down and saw the distance he had made between the two of them. Putting his hands in his pockets, he leaned back on the bed of rock and looked back at the mountains. He exhaled and a puff of hot breath was visible to him.

When Jessica made it to him they continued upwards at her pace. This wasn't frustrating to Anthony. He had used up his excited burst and felt more aware of these new surroundings he wanted to acquaint himself with. Wet and muddy now, he had broken a seal that hadn't often even been scratched since childhood. It made the muck and puddles sprinkled randomly across the rock path upward not obstacles to be avoided at the risk of needing to wash his clothing, but instead something he could enjoy and explore. He gripped and stared with a more concentrated and intimate eye up the hill while Jessica continued to praise the beauty of the view that was now behind them.

The top came. When Anthony put his foot on the flat surface of the little plateau, a gust of wind hit him in the face. He cursed and ducked down, waddling onto into more secure ground.

"Careful coming up," He said to Jessica. "The wind's strong. It almost blew me back."

Jessica's head was the only thing visible to Anthony. But she nodded and crouched down like he had and walked next to him. The two stood up and steadied themselves while the wind beat at them. They were standing on the large stone. At the end of the stone was a foot drop into some patchy grass and dirt before another fall that would land in a massive river. The current didn't seem strong but Anthony knew he was too high up to tell.

There was a small tour standing in the patch below the rock. Their guide was shouting over the wind about the immediate area. Anthony and Jessica tried to listen but were both too distracted by the enrapturing landscape. The trees below them were bare but somehow on the other side of the river were encompassing patches of multi-colored foliage. In the water were blocks of ice that had broken off from the larger mass of it upriver. Some of the ice moved slowly while others appeared stationary as a miniature example of what was ahead. Anthony and Jessica waited here for the tour to get a little distance on them then moved on themselves.

The path was now sandwiched between a larger mountain and trees that blocked the view of the river. The trees staved off the wind slightly.

"How much do you think we've done." Jessica asked as Anthony hopped over a puddle.

"I don't think we've gone far." He replied, turning around to help her over with his hands. "We've only gone up."

"But it wasn't straight up." Jessica argued.

"Yeah, but I think in the ten minutes we've been walking along the river. We've gone further across than that whole climb."

"Maybe, how far do you think we've gone?"

"I don't think we're almost done."

"I don't think we are either. I'm just curious. What do you think?"

"Maybe a mile at the most. In like linear distance."

"Thank you, that sounds right to me."

A little further on, the tress on their left got thicker and others began springing out from the mountainside. Eventually they couldn't feel the wind and it felt like they were strolling through the woods more than through a mountain path. There was a stream running down from the mountain that went through their woodsy path, bridged by the trunk of a tree. They sat on the rocks around it that formed a natural rest stop.

"Can we sit here a bit?" Anthony asked.

"What?" Jessica asked back, teasingly, "Are you tired?"

"No," He answered anyway. "I just want to sit here a minute."

He was watching the water in the stream pass him, picking out and focusing on the leaves, twigs, and pines that were drifting down. The sand under the clear water reminded him of the sand from the pond he used to walk to as a child. It had a similar color. This whole area looked like it could've been lifted out of the woods that surrounded his old pond. Maybe if he had come here as a child he would have gotten a greater appreciation for this stream. He definitely had appreciated his humble nameless woods back then more than this place now. Before he could've seen life and stories behind the floating discards of nature. Now it just reminded him of trash littering a city like the one lived in now.

"Ready to go?" He asked.

She handed him a bag of trail mix. "Eat some of this first. We might be close to halfway already."

He took the bag and ate a little before the two walked over the wide trunk. The trail began to slope upward again but this area was dusty and easier to get up. They were on the peak. Directly in front of them was another mountain that was substantially higher. The couple looked at each other and laughed before climbing down the still dusty mountain path and scaling the higher one. The wind had returned before they reached the second peak and must have been tunneled and made stronger by concentration in the space between the two mountains. Heading up the second mountain was a push against the wind and they were tired by the time they reached the top. They couldn't stop because even though they were sweating, the air and wind was freezing enough at this height to make them immediately start to shiver. After a small climb down was another plateau they could walk along, where the wind continued to blow in their face only slightly more softly. The river was on their left again. There was more ice in the water. They came to a decline in the land that brought them down into another forest. At the beginning of the way down was a wooden sign.

"Oh, it's got a map on it." Jessica shouted over the wind, walking in front of Anthony.

She looked at the map and groaned loudly before Anthony could see the sign. On the far left of the wood was the first camp and on the far right was where they were going. The star indicating their location was about a quarter way across.

"Look though," Anthony said, trying to make his tired girlfriend feel better. "We go up three times total and we've already gone up twice. So we're about to get a lot closer as we walk down the mountain and through the woods."

"Yeah, but the next elevation is the highest," She whined.

"Do you want to stop and rest?" Anthony asked.

She nodded. "Let's wait to feel cold then keep moving."

Anthony took off his bag and sat on it. His assurances had been almost as much for him as her. He could be a lot stronger.

Jessica sat next to him in the same way and they started eating more trail mix and drinking from their bottles. A few minutes after the break had started, a hawk flew down and landed in front of them.

"That thing is huge!" Anthony exclaimed as he met his girlfriend's surprised eyes.

Jessica nodded. "Yeah, what do you think it's doing?"

"Maybe it's tired from flying in the wind." Anthony said.

The hawk did seem to be resting with its head tucked into its brown wild and ruffled feathers. A few seconds later its sharp beak reemerged. It looked at the couple with its intense eyes then took off.

"The poor thing!" Jessica laughed. The hawk was being blown backwards. Anthony felt a little guilty happiness in his aching muscles at the wild animal's difficulty adjusting to the elements. His condolence was short lived though when the hawk took a dip down, which somehow allowed it to beautifully cut through the wind, across to the other mountain.

"Wow," Jessica cooed. "That was beautiful."

"Imagine being that free." Anthony.

"Part of being out here I guess." Jessica said, her mood now drastically improved. "Ready to get going again?"

Anthony smiled and nodded.

"Do you need another second?" Jessica asked.

"No," Anthony replied, getting up, telling his still aching body it had to improve.

Snow country. That was the name of this place. And it fit. Ryan felt back home as he trudged through he deep powder to the sidewalks, which were kept clean of the falling fat white flakes by little hoses releasing water hot enough to make steam to rise when it hit the ground that must have been connected to the hot springs. It was a short walk to his inn. Once he arrived, he checked in and went to the small shrine on the top floor, which was just a room that had been kept in the old style adorned with pictures of the great writer. Ryan looked at the pictures of the writer and the people who had been close to him here with his copy in his hand. After, he read in the chair just outside the special room.

Here

The day was warm. It was the first one of Spring. There was still plenty of snow separating the streets from the sidewalks, but now it was melting and changing back from the gross hard substance he had trudged through during the hardest months of winter back to the beautiful light charm that had been falling when he first arrived.

The beauty of the snow was clearest from his seat. From the bench he took in how the pure coating lined the tops of the knee high bamboo fences that segregated the slushy paths from the blanketed yard. It was a nice addition to the castle also, covering each level's crown-like roof in white contrasting the black wood body of the castle shaded by each roof.

The sky above the castle was clear and blue so he could see the mountains beyond the town. He wasn't looking at the mountains. He wasn't really looking at anything. His mind felt a satisfying heaviness and his eyelids hovered above being close. The pull he had felt on arrival had gone. He missed it in a way, the first feeling. But he knew it was better gone. It had become heavy after awhile and then suddenly empty. That had been the hard part from both the drop and the uncertainty. He was glad that it was over. Not because he had finished the naive and vain quest for enlightenment he had first set out on, but simply because he was comfortable.

The day felt hotter than it was. The sun was bright and warm so the rays reflected off the snow, giving it a hazy quality that reminded him the snow was melting. The streets would look strange without it. But they were the same as would be his routine. The difference in season here was now as superfluous as a haircut. It was good to be here and not because it was exciting, or new, or enlightening, or valuable.

Only because this was his home.

His two bags were packed again. He was proud that he hadn't needed more room. It was time to go.

In the Park's Shade

Ryan Clarke was twenty-eight years old

Sunlight was peeking through the sparse branches. It was fall, but felt like summer to Ryan, making comparisons with the March temperature back home difficult to avoid. He was probably a little sunburnt. He had taken too long to get in the shade. Even if he was, the burn wouldn't last long and was a good price for finding a place like this to put down his bag and stretch out on the grass. His fingers absentmindedly caressed the book laying next to his backpack, which caused the pages to lift into a curve and then fall with a satisfying ticking sound. Ryan pulled the bag closer to him to use as a pillow and closed his eyes. He wasn't particularly tired. Walking in the sun and heat had caused him to sweat a lot, mostly under his jeans and where his bag covered his back. That had always made Ryan a sort of sleepy and lethargic. But lethargic was too negative a word. His feeling was a wholesome one through peace, which made him acutely aware of the small happenings around him like the soft noise of the swaying branches above him or the manic movements of squirrels across them. It was all he needed to occupy his mind sitting in the park.

It wasn't a very beautiful park. There was a lot of discarded litter, panhandling homeless, and a main road along one of its sides that polluted tranquility with its traffic. Ryan still had more than he needed here. He was content to lay in the park for the rest of the afternoon. He had his book. He had lunch. And most importantly, he had a weightlessness in his mind.

Even if the temperature dropped or it started to rain it wouldn't matter. This place, like all the others he had lived in since leaving home had a much softer idea of what was bad weather or cold. He had probably gotten little too used to the warmer temperatures and lost some of the grit he had unknowingly developed growing up, but he still wouldn't be uncomfortable. Ryan had decided early in his life abroad that it had been a blessing to be callous to the cold. There was a well-roundedness to a person who used the cold for invigoration and then enjoyed heat for pleasure that satisfied the amateur stoic philosophy he had been building for himself since he had started hitting heavy-bags years ago. A train of thought Ryan had been happy to learn was somewhat mirrored by Aristotle.

Feeling the presence of someone approaching, Ryan opened his eyes and saw a bedraggled man coming up to him holding a box. The man asked if Ryan wanted candy bars in heavily dialect-Spanish. Feeling generous, even though he didn't eat what he offered anymore, gave the man a bill and held his hand up to block the transaction of returning his coins for change. The man thanked him and moved on to the young couple vigorously kissing on top of each other not far from Ryan.

Deciding this was as good a time to eat, Ryan opened the smaller of the two pouches on his bag and took out the smaller brown paper one and his golden water bottle. A stray dog approached him as he ate. They were numerous in both the park and the city in general. This had been difficult to see at first. He had considered stray dogs a product of a sadder dirtier past. He realized now that that way of thinking had been ignorance on his home's resources, which came with an unsettling suspicion to the motivation behind the utilization of those resources when he would watch these ragged but docile animals function without causing much issue in this society.

His new friend was big with light brown fur and a retriever's face distinguishable through his mix. He had tan patches of his fur from needing a bath and a sad nick in his left ear. The dog did not look sad. He had lay down close to Ryan, resting his chin in the grass. Sometimes he would look at Ryan. He wasn't begging. Instead, showing the comfortable companionship between a human and dog.

Ryan ripped off a part of his sandwich and tossed it in the dog's direction. It landed a few inches from the dog's nose and he craned his neck forward to snap it up without suspicion. Now finished with his food, Ryan put his water bottle back in his bag and left the disposal of his brown bag for after he got up. Pulling his backpack behind his head to prop it up, Ryan thumped the ground with a flat hand and the dog got up and came closer to Ryan. Scratching the dog's head as he read his book, Ryan felt more at peace.

He saw Maria approaching through the people in the park as his eyes drifted curiously above his book. She was late. This didn't matter in any way but to be comical to Ryan for the consistency of this trait. She had seen him first and was disappointed she hadn't been fast enough to sneak up on him. Sitting up, Ryan waited for her to get close and put his book down and his hands out happily to greet her.

"How's your day been?" She asked taking his hands. She was small and tan with brown hair and green eyes. She was also an American. But she was sometimes mistaken for a local.

Especially since it was a trend here for men who looked liked Ryan to date local women. Ryan liked her. It wasn't her first time living abroad either. Familiarity had been the first of many things that had made them connect.

"It's been relaxing." Ryan answered. "Did you get everything done?"

She nodded as she sat down next to him, guided by his hands. "I finished planning my lessons while I was at the laundromat." She leaned against Ryan and put her head on his shoulder. "I still have to fold. It's all in a pile on my bed. But that seemed like a nighttime problem."

"Why didn't you just do it." Ryan laughed before kissing her on the side of the head. "You already did most of it."

"Leave me alone." She groaned, playfully knocking her forehead against Ryan's lightly. "I'll get to it." Then she kissed him. They kissed hard for a long time. Like the couple near them, and numerous others throughout the park, they allowed the more permissible rules of public affection in Latin America separate them from everything but each other. Ryan put his arms around her as they separated and pulled her down into the grass playfully, making Maria giggle. He squeezed tightly and pecked this somehow familiar girls face in the park across the street from his home.

Ryan was happy.

The sun had sunk. The noise city had begun to change. Ryan lay in his bed looking out the windows as his view of the Andes faded. When he couldn't see them anymore, he got up to go into his kitchen and make his dinner.

Buoy

I was back home. After promising for months, the end of summer had guilted me into not just coming down but also bringing my friends as an extra apologetic offering to my mother. And now, for the first time in years, I was rocking in the choppy water on a surfboard. My knees hung off each side of the fiberglass with the rest of my legs submerged in the dark water. I didn't feel cold. And I shouldn't. It was a hot August day so the ocean didn't get much warmer.

Still, getting into the water had been embarrassing hops in and out of the receding waves before my legs and feet stopped stinging. Then I was able to wade into the shallows and climb onto the board, paddling chest raised in order to keep the rest of me dry a little longer. My upper half's exposure had been much quicker, but more traumatic. After being thrown from the board while trying to pop up, the water had shocked me into a twitchy still and I felt heavy floating limply in the ocean. The process had started off familiarly. I had picked out a bump in the water that I thought would form better than those that had been before, tilted the board slightly to the right to better accommodate my *goofy-foot* stance, then started paddling. When the wave started to propel me faster than I ever could, I had jumped up. But instead of both feet landing neatly, I received a painful knee bash when one foot missed. I lifted a knee to try and salvage the situation but my balance was thrown. Then once the soaking's shock had faded, the disappointment at my skill's deterioration set in.

Now I was bobbing. My upper half was almost dry. Another wave momentarily lifted me up and let me down as it passed, like a rocking buoy keeping its place through oceanic turbulence. That was a leftover analogy from when I had started surfing. Being young, the comparison had seemed funny. Now a buoy's obstruction to the seascape was a more prevalent thought. Grossly bright zits attracting the eye to their little spot due to their misplacement in the beautiful sea, never moving anywhere, just bobbing in a place that wasn't really theirs. Feeling this same misplacement with my supposed sport was the sobering final push my mind needed to retire its use as a character trait.

This newfound self-awareness was followed by an unease during the lifts and lowers that regressed me even further than I had ever been, reminding me I was floating isolated in the ocean, deep in the territory of what by all intents and purposes were monsters. I started to stare at the water below and focused to make out my swaying feet, unable to see anything deeper than that.

Because there was probably nothing. I reminded myself.

As if on cue, a sea lion poked its head out about ten yards to the left. We made eye contact as the large, dark, grizzled animal sunk back underwater. I swallowed. The fight to only think like a tourist barely lasted a few seconds and I leaned defensively forward on the board so my legs could take safety on the back end.

Folding my arms to make a pillow for my head, I scanned the area the sea lion had emerged from, barely acknowledging Patrick paddling up.

"Made it to shore on that last one." Patrick said, happily. "Took some knocks getting back out here though. What? Did you wipe-out?"

"Yeah, barely got up. Went to one knee then got thrown off."

Patrick laughed, nicely, "I guess you'd be a little rusty." Then noticing my stiffness on the board, asked, "It's not bumming you out, is it?"

"Nah," I replied, sitting up and forcing my feet back in the water, "I was just staring at where I saw a sea lion. Thought maybe he'd pop back up again."

"Oh yeah," Patrick said, stretching his arms above his head. "That's cool. It's really been awhile for you, huh?" Then he pointed at dark blubbery flesh coming out of the water about ten yards to his left, saying through a yawn, "There he is." Before the tail followed its torso back into the other world.

Nodding, I turned the board back to shore before the shape had completely disappeared again.

"And down he goes." Patrick said, goofily. My friend had aged well. He was still thin, but years of landscaping had built his muscles up to a statuesque physique. An image complimented by his olive tan that was at its deepest this time of year. He had grown out his once buzzed blonde hair and it was curly at the tips. The biggest differences that had come in the time between our early and late twenties were artificial, tattoos and a scar. One tattoo was on his back. It was a basic one, the area code we were in. The second was over his left pectoral of an intricately drawn skull with its mouth open in a way to show it was laughing, which deteriorated both literally and in detail from one end to the other. That was the only intimidating thing about Patrick and his scar was the only ugly one. It was in the middle of his right pectoral. About two inches in vertical length, the thin lesion stood out from the puffing that came from neglectful healing. But Patrick wasn't self conscious. He was too beautiful to be. He had only talked with me about that scar once and over the last few years had trusted me to let him lie to other people about it.

I looked over my shoulder at each wave rolling towards me. Picking the third one away as the mark, I waited for the two preceding to pass before laying flat and starting to paddle. I heard encouraging shouts from Patrick as I picked up speed. Lifting slightly to the top of the rushing water, I jumped up. This time landing on both feet but slipping backwards on both heels.

Finding myself underwater again, I let out a gargled scream once I had fought with the underwater current and locked in position. I resurfaced and swam along the leash to my old board and hoisted myself back onto it. I was steady again in time to see Patrick jump off his board near the shore.

The beach was pretty full. We were the only two on surf-boards. There were several boogie-boarders near the sandbar intermingled with the swimmers and body-surfers. My friends were on their towels, waiting to go for a casual swim once I was done here. It was something they had suggested earlier because *'we could all do it together'*.

I hoped they were enjoying themselves. They probably were. One of the aspects of growing up here was I still saw the beach fundamentally different than my more suburban friends. Going to the beach was a bigger deal to them, a defining day. But to me it was really closer to how they would see going to the park.

Patrick was already about halfway back. He had been an interesting specimen to my guests. *'A more Chris-version of Chris'* they had said with happy chuckles, seeing the mannerisms the city hadn't yet squeezed out of me in everything he did. That association had been perplexing and even a little disturbing because it had at first seemed to me like Patrick hadn't changed in the years since I left home. But that wasn't true. He had improved. He had taken a more chronological course that had the benefit of tangibly related steps. A benefit I couldn't enjoy. If I could enjoy any at all. The reality was I had gambled the skills that had come naturally throughout my childhood and those chips had already been scooped up, raising the question of whether I had won anything with the costly ante?

I couldn't do Patrick's job and Patrick couldn't do mine but Patrick had worked his way to comfort. Whatever had convinced me that deviating from the work inherent here would make me happy, I could not remember.

Patrick was almost back. A wave was picking up behind me. Without looking, I went down and started paddling. The board started moving fast so I pushed down and popped my knees up. It was frustrating having to tell my body what it was sure it remembered was wrong. My toes touched down on the board in near synchronization and I came up wobbling, before rolling forward into the surf.

About the Author

Jonathan Maniscalco has taught English to ESL learners in Japan, Spain, Chile, and New York City. A Massachusetts native, he is a graduate of Boston University and is currently completing a Master's Degree at Clark University. *15 Stories to Home* is his second published short story collection. His first novel, *The Dog Star Burned* will be published in 2021."